M000072931

The Day After

By Andrew Baze

Max Publications

First Edition: May 2014

The characters and events in this book are fictitious. Any similarity to real persons, living or dead, is coincidental and not intended by the author. At the time of writing, all call signs referenced in the book either had permission of the license-holder or were unissued.

Introduction – Read Me!

Dear Reader,

In this book, you'll notice something uncommon to most adventure novels: the use of endnotes. These endnotes are organized in the **Bonus Content** section at the end of the novel. If you see a word with a small number next to it, flip to the Bonus Content section, look up that number, and you'll be able to learn more about that topic.

Also, please keep this in mind: getting involved with amateur radio is fun and easy! If you're not sure where to start, just follow these four simple steps:

1) **Get a book** that will help you prepare for the basic ("Technician") license. Don't worry – it's not difficult. A good place to find a study guide is www.ARRL.org.
2) **Take the test and get your license!**
3) **Buy a handheld amateur radio.** Good news: you can probably find one new for under $50!
4) **Get on the air!** For example, you can talk with someone on a local repeater, get involved with a ham club in your area, or even drill with an emergency communications team. Get on the air and give it a try. You'll love it!

This page is also a good reference to help you get licensed: www.ARRL.org/getting-licensed.

Do you want more tips on ham radio, emergency communications, urban survival, disaster preparedness, and other interesting topics? Go to www.PreparedBlog.com and www.EmergencyCommunicationsBlog.com, and you'll find articles, general tips, more details about topics found in this book, pictures, links, and other cool stuff!

I hope you love the story and learn from the extra details.

73,
-Andrew Baze
AB8L

Chapter 1

"Hold on, it feels like there's an elephant walking down the hallway," Katy said, holding her cell phone away from her ear, trying to pinpoint the source of the thumping.

The floor jumped. The scenery outside moved. As Katy staggered, trying to keep her balance, she heard screams and shouts from down the hall. A large window near her shattered, and air rushed out. The howling air and the building's groaning combined into an orchestra of destructive noise, and then everything went black.

***

Katy lay face-down on the floor. The industrial carpet offered no padding, and she ached all over. She tried to open her eyes. Her left eye opened easily, but the right one was stuck shut. And her head hurt. This was a lot different than a headache the morning after staying out too late with her band.

She gingerly brushed the crust away from her eye, then slowly opened it. Her vision was normal, although it was difficult to be sure in the near darkness. Trying to identify the source of the headache, she felt around her forehead and scalp, wincing when she found the wound. That must be what had gummed up her eye – blood from a gash on her scalp.

Katy continued her self-assessment, moving as little as possible, trying to determine whether she had any other injuries. It didn't feel like anything was missing or broken, but it was hard to be sure, because she was numb in places. Then she finally realized how cold she was.

She rolled stiffly to her side and sat up slowly, paying attention to all of her joints as she moved. Her head hurt even worse now, and a wave of nausea rolled over her. She took a slow, deep breath, then another. That felt a little better. Good, she probably hadn't lost too much blood. But she was really thirsty. She looked around again in the near darkness, slowly coming back to her senses. Then she remembered.

Hours earlier, she had been at work, sitting in the break area and using her cell phone. It was a perfect place for a quiet, private conversation, unlike in her cubicle, where everyone could hear her.

Then the shaking started, and the swaying. Her employer leased the entire 27th floor of the high-rise, and at this height, it felt like she had been at the top of a tall tree in a windstorm, as the building whipped from side to side. She remembered screaming, crashing, and then everything went black.

Katy realized it must have been an earthquake. She'd heard for years that the Seattle was due to have "the big one" at any time, and apparently it had been time.

What time was it anyhow? She looked at her watch. She couldn't make it out in the low light, so she pressed a button on the side, lighting up the display. 4:32. She blinked and looked at the digital readout more closely. 4:32 A.M. What the heck had happened? She slowly looked around, and realized she was alone. Where was everybody?

Still collecting her wits, she looked around on the floor until she spotted it. Her cell phone lay only a few feet away, visible in the pre-dawn glow coming through what was left of the nearby windows. It lay near a pile of shattered safety glass. A gentle breeze blew through the gaping hole and she shivered violently. That's why she was so cold. She scooped up the phone and saw the battery was nearly dead. She checked more closely and realized it didn't matter. The signal display area that usually showed several bars now showed a "No signal" symbol. That was a bad sign. Then one more indicator caught her eye, the message icon with the number "1" next to it. She had an unread text message. It must have come through after the quake, but before the cell towers had gone offline.

With slow, cold fingers, Katy opened the message. It was from her boyfriend Lucas. "I'm OK. Are U? Where R U?" Reflexively, she clumsily replied, "I'm alive. Where R U? I'm heading home now from work." She hit "Send" and watched closely. Would it go through? "No signal, try again?" flashed on the screen. She was disappointed, but not surprised. Something big enough to shake this building was certainly big enough to disrupt cell service.

She took another look around in the dim light and saw the shape of a large, fluorescent light fixture on the floor next to her. She stood up carefully and looked around again. Chairs were tipped over and many of the ceiling tiles lay on the floor. It looked like a hurricane had blown through. It must have been a huge earthquake, to cause this much damage in a new building. And that fixture next to her was probably what had hit her on the head, which is why she had been unconscious for... She looked at her watch again, and thought back to when the quake had hit. She had been unconscious for over sixteen hours!

Now that her head was finally clearing, Katy finally noticed the incredible pressure in her bladder. She was surprised she hadn't wet herself while lying there so long. Quickly, she opened her smartphone's flashlight application. Thankfully, the phone still had enough battery power left to operate the LED light on the back, and it clearly illuminated her path. As fast as she could, she made her way to the bathroom. She pushed the door open and stepped in. Aside from the light her phone radiated, it was black. It looked a little creepy, but Katy didn't care. All she cared about now was emptying her bladder.

Katy darted into a stall and took care of business, wondering how she'd lasted so long during the previous day and night without using the bathroom. Her pants weren't wet, but there was no way she could have lasted that long without going to the bathroom. Then she remembered, vaguely, trying to stand up in the dark with a splitting headache, taking a couple halting steps, and she had peed. But where? It couldn't have been too far away, since she'd woken up in the break area. Well, she had no intention of looking for a puddle anywhere. Nobody would notice when they remodeled the whole thing someday. The important thing was that she woke up with dry pants.

Done with her reminiscing and grateful for the real toilet, she completed her task. When she stepped away from the toilet, she noticed that it didn't flush as it usually did. The automatic sensor wasn't working. Of course, she realized. The sensor used electricity, and this building had none. But she had much bigger concerns now, and nobody was going to care about an unflushed toilet.[1]

It wasn't all bad. The building still had water pressure. There must be a water storage tank on an upper floor somewhere, she thought, as she washed her hands and looked in the mirror. In the dim light of her cell phone, she was a grisly sight, with dried blood streaking her forehead and face. She looked like an actress in a low-budget horror movie, a zombie who hadn't started decomposing yet. She grabbed some paper towels, wet them in the sink, gently lifted her hair away from the wound, and dabbed at the area. Now that she could see the cut more closely, she realized it was minor, about an inch long but not very deep. Hopefully it wouldn't need stitches. With a little more effort, she was able to get more of the blood out of her thick, dark brown hair. She pulled it back into a loose pony tail, using one of the hair ties she always carried in her pocket. After cleaning her face more, she took another quick look in the mirror. The wound was still exposed, but she looked human again.

Katy left the bathroom and went back to the kitchen area. It was a mess. The violent shaking had caused the cupboards to vomit most of their contents onto the floor. But the first aid cabinet mounted to the wall next to the sink was still securely latched shut. She opened it and took out small boxes of antiseptic wipes, antibiotic cream, painkillers, medical tape and bandages, setting them on the nearby counter. With another quick trip to the bathroom mirror, the techniques she'd practiced in her Red Cross first aid course last year came back to her quickly as she finished cleaning the wound, then applied butterfly strips[2] and an additional bandage, to cover the wound site. The last thing she needed now was an infection. Stepping back from the mirror, she surveyed her work proudly. With the flesh-colored bandage, the wound was hardly noticeable.

Pangs of thirst caught up with her again. She found a clean-looking cup on the floor in the break area, rinsed it in the kitchen sink and filled it with water. She drank it all without stopping. Then she tore open a small pack of ibuprofen and chased the two red pills with another cup of water. She filled the cup again and took a deep breath. She had to figure out what to do next. She needed a plan.

Katy hadn't ever been in a situation like this before. She'd seen all kinds of interesting disasters in the movies, but knew most of it wouldn't be useful in real life.

Fortunately, Katy had a unique skill that was useful in real life, and she was paid to use it every day. She was a project manager and actually enjoyed organizing and planning. She knew that taking extra time to create a good plan was usually much more effective than jumping into something with a limited plan, or no plan at all, which is what many of her coworkers seemed to prefer. It was Katy's nature to plan.

She walked to a nearby whiteboard and found a marker on the floor nearby. She wrote:

- *Goal 1: Get out of building*
- *Goal 2: Get home – Car? On foot?*
- *Need: Water, light, radio, medical supplies → my car?*
- *Next steps: Go down, assess*
- *Drive or walk home*

That was enough. It wasn't a big plan, but it was something written down, and Katy felt a lot more organized.

She walked back toward the cubicles. Many partitions lay on the ground. Bookshelves and filing cabinets had tipped over, adding their contents to the mess.

Making her way carefully to what was left of her work area with her phone lighting the way, Katy eventually found her desk. She jerked opened the side drawer and smiled as she saw what she was hoping to find: her purse. She opened it, retrieved her flashlight and clicked it on. It put out over 100 lumens[3] and lit up much of the area. Then she turned off the cell phone to conserve its battery, and stowed it in the purse.

Katy took a moment to shine her flashlight around. It was an unsettling scene. All of the things that had seemed so important to her the day before were in complete disarray. Her TPS reports were spread all over the floor, her computer had tipped over, and her monitor lay face down on the desk. Everything seemed sideways or upside down. And for the foreseeable future, all of this stuff was worthless. It was surreal.

She went back to the kitchen and found a garbage can. She pulled out the dirty bag and looked underneath. As she suspected, the cleaning staff had left some clean bags under the dirty one, so they'd be available the next time the can was emptied. She took two of them, opened them and put one inside of the other.

Then she went back to the pile of first aid contents she'd taken out earlier and stuffed them in the bag. The odds were good she'd need them or would find someone else who needed them, and they wouldn't do anyone any good here.

Katy left the bag on the floor and went around the corner to where office supplies were stored. She scanned the floor for a moment until she found the weapon she'd sought. She returned to the break area, where the vending machine stood. Given the circumstances, she didn't feel bad about what she was about to do. She reared back and threw the heavy tape dispenser into the glass.

Katy carefully plucked out several remaining glass shards. Then she proceeded to collect chips, beef jerky, candy bars and trail mix, glad that she and her coworkers had requested some healthy food options the year before. While sugar and fat tasted great, she would need more than junk food for fuel today. She stopped for a few seconds to wolf down a bag of nuts and raisins, followed by a handful of Skittles. It wasn't yoghurt and granola like she was used to, but it was a source of quick calories, and she knew she'd need them.

The soda vending machine was another story. There was no glass face to break, and she had no idea how to open it. She searched on the ground by the cupboards, until she found three empty, plastic water containers, swag from some company event. She filled them at the faucet, closed the lids tightly, put two in the garbage bag and one in her purse.

Almost ready to start her downward trek, Katy quickly peered out a broken window. Twenty-seven floors below, she saw a horrible mess. The streets were littered with abandoned cars and covered with broken glass and rubble from the surrounding buildings. She looked from side to side. To the north, she saw a tall office building with flames flickering in several windows about halfway up. Thankfully, she didn't see anyone in the windows above the level of the fire. Hopefully everyone had already escaped.

Next to the building on fire, two older buildings had collapsed completely. The people in those buildings probably hadn't been so lucky, she thought grimly. Pulling her eyes away from the destruction, she scanned to the east, toward her home. She saw several columns of smoke, and the glow of flames below them.

Lowering her gaze from the horizon, she looked down to the highway, Interstate 405, which passed by less than a hundred yards away from the building. The bridge that usually spanned the highway was gone. Instead, a pile of twisted wreckage lay on the highway below where the bridge used to cross. Stationary cars lined up on the right side in the northbound lane and on the left side in the southbound lane. Many appeared to have crashed into each other. Some had burned and smoke still drifted lazily from their blackened shells. But she didn't see any people. Where was everyone? Maybe people were waiting for the sun to finish rising before braving their new reality.

This was worse than she had expected. It also meant that Lucas was probably out of the equation for at least a couple days. Since he lived and worked in West Seattle, many miles and at least two major bridges away from her work and home, the odds were slim that they would be able to connect in person anytime in the near future. He would probably be busy trying to survive on his own. She hoped his neighborhood wasn't wrecked.

After they'd been dating for a couple of months, when Katy brought up the subject of disaster preparedness and amateur radio, Lucas made it clear he wasn't interested in either topic. She'd let it go. And for now, he might as well be in Siberia. He'd have to fight this battle on his own.

Katy thought about her car. It was on level P-5, a full five floors underground. Looking at the condition of the streets and the highway, she knew that even if she were able to get her car out of the garage, she wouldn't be able to drive out of this area.

But it still had things she needed. Katy put off the decision to go underground until she saw what the ground floor looked like.

The elevators were useless. Even if they had been powered, they would have automatically lowered themselves to the ground floor. So Katy opened the door to the stairwell, stepped onto the landing, and shined her flashlight up and down. Although her work area looked like a hurricane had blown through, the stairwell appeared to have weathered the earthquake undamaged. She started downward.

Katy often spent several minutes on the stairs before lunch, walking the twenty-seven floors down. She took more than twice as long today, descending cautiously.

The stairwell smelled and sounded different than usual. Katy realized the usual hum of the air conditioning fans was absent, leaving the air stagnant but warm. A few floors down, Katy finally felt warm on the inside, the last of the chill dispelled by her physical activity. Then she finally reached the ground floor and pushed open the door.

Chapter 2

Robbie ran down the narrow path, fighting a feeling of impending doom that weighed him down more with every step. His father was stranded on the side of a cliff, seriously injured and waiting for help. Robbie also knew that his mother and sister were in danger, huddled in terror at home, so far away. He felt their fear and it amplified his own. He thundered down the hiking trail toward his father's truck, gasping for breath.

Moments later, legs and lungs burning, he rounded a bend in the trail and saw the truck, only about fifty yards away. He gathered his last energy reserves and picked up the pace.

Robbie felt the ground shake again. He tried to keep running, but could barely keep his balance. Without warning, a massive crack opened in the ground just in front of him, completely crossing the trail. Robbie fell, sliding forward and trying to stop, but his momentum carried him forward.

Scrabbling for a handhold, he slid over the edge, plummeting into the chasm. Robbie stopped breathing as he fell into the void, looking up at the rapidly-receding sky as it was replaced by blackness.

***

Gasping for breath, Robbie sat up with a jerk and looked around wildly. Realizing where he was, he unclenched his fists.

As his brain adjusted to his new reality, he slowed his breathing and tried to relax. He was in his bed. He was safe. It had been a dream.

The experiences of the previous day had resulted in a long night of tossing and turning, and it felt like he'd only fallen asleep a half hour ago. Maybe he had. It was hard to tell, without being able to consult the normal green glow of the electric alarm clock on his nightstand.

His previous day had been the craziest in his fourteen years. It had started before dawn, and he hadn't slept well the night before either, because he had been so excited to go camping in the mountains with his father. But their trip had been cut short by a massive earthquake, and they'd spent the rest of the day slowly navigating their way home, through the wreckage and chaos.

Getting home was just the first set of hurdles they'd overcome. A terrifying series of events was already unfolding even as they were pulling into the driveway, and Robbie's quick thinking had saved his mother and sister, and put a bad man behind bars. At least, they hoped he was behind bars. It had taken more than three hours and two radio calls to the emergency operations center for an exhausted police officer to come by and pick the man up, and that was only because Robbie's father, Jeff, knew the officer from his softball league.

Eventually the mood in the household calmed, and there was much hugging combined with a few tears of relief. But the excitement of the day translated into a poor night's sleep.

In any case, it was daytime now, and time to get rolling. Still wiping sleep from his eyes, Robbie trudged down the stairs and into the kitchen. His mother and father, Marie and Jeff, were sitting at the kitchen table, talking quietly. On the table next to them sat a teakettle, perched on a butane camp stove. It started to whistle gently, as if to announce his entrance.

"Mornin'," Robbie mumbled. Jeff and Marie both looked up and smiled at him.

"Good morning, Robbie," Marie said, turning off the stove. "Come here. Did you sleep well? How are you feeling?" She stood up and held out her arms. Robbie's mother usually wasn't very talkative first thing in the morning, at least until after she'd had a cup of coffee, but these were unusual times.

Robbie walked over and hugged her. Jeff stepped over and hugged them both, and they all stood quietly for a moment.

"Let's have some coffee," Jeff said.

Marie got mugs from the cupboard, spooned in some instant coffee, and filled the mugs with hot water. She pushed a mug toward Robbie.

"Coffee?" Robbie asked, cocking one eyebrow quizzically. He had inherited that ability from his mother. "Since when do I drink coffee?"

"You might as well have a grown-up drink," Jeff said. "You really proved yourself yesterday. Your mom and I are proud of you. And it's a reminder."

"Of what?" Robbie asked, taking the mug.

"Keep thinking like an adult. We were lucky to make it home, and the women are lucky we made it home when we did. In fact, we're lucky to still have a home. We don't know how long it's going to be before things are back to normal, and other problems will come up. You'll have to solve some of them on your own. Stay smart. Make sense?"

"I guess," Robbie replied. He recognized his dad's "I'm teaching you something, so pay attention" look, and responded with his own thoughtful nod. Then he grinned. "Hey, I thought you said that caffeine is a drug, and it'll stunt my growth."

"That's true," Jeff replied with a matching grin. "That's why you got decaf."

"Then what's the point?" Robbie asked. He took a sip and made a sour face. "By the way, this tastes gross."

14

"The point is that you have more common sense than a lot of adults do. So use it. Please, please, please use your head and stay safe."

"OK, Dad." It sounded like Jeff was over-doing it a bit. But he could tell his father really cared about him and only wanted him to be safe, so he went along with it. It could be worse. Sometimes, his friends would tell Robbie stories about how their dads acted. Some of them sounded like real jerks. Some weren't even around anymore. This wasn't so bad.

Robbie tried another sip. "Blech. Do you have some chocolate syrup or something?"

"Nope. That stuff is nothing but corn syrup anyway. Probably worse for you than caffeine would be. Drink your coffee like a man. We have a lot to do today. Are you ready to help me check out the neighborhood?" Jeff asked.

"Sure, after I get dressed. What's the plan?" He pushed the mug away and grabbed a piece of buttered bread.

"We have a lot of assessing to do. Now you're going to see why I've worked so hard to get our neighbors on board with CERT and the other disaster preparedness stuff. I've been up most of the night, getting started with some of the neighbors. A lot of them are probably going to need help this morning, now that there's no electricity. I'll be the one coordinating efforts, so I have to get back to my radio now. More people will be checking in. We have at least a few more neighbors I'm hoping to hear from, if they're using the calling clock, like Mr. Ellison from around the corner, and Katy from next door. I would have expected to hear from her by now. She wasn't home when I checked, so she's probably out in the city somewhere. I need to be there if they radio in."

"Eat this," Marie said, pushing a bowl of cereal and milk in front of Robbie. She handed him a Clif bar. "And stick this in your pocket for later. You'll probably be hungry again soon."

"Mom?" All eyes turned as five-year-old Lisa appeared at the bottom of the stairs, pausing unsteadily, her eyes half-open.

"Hey baby," Marie said, and sweeping her up in a hug and planting a big kiss on her cheek. "How about some breakfast." Another bowl of cereal appeared. Marie poured milk into it and set it in front of Lisa, with a spoon.

"I'm glad you're OK, Robbie," Lisa said, with her mouth full. We were scared for you and Daddy." Robbie looked embarrassed.

"I'm glad you're OK too, Lisa." She looked OK. He was glad that the ordeal didn't appear to have traumatized her. Impulsively, he got to his feet, walked over and gave her a hug.

She hugged him back, then shoveled another huge spoonful of cereal into her mouth. A trail of milk dribbled down her chin. He grinned and hugged her again.

Chapter 3

Katy opened the door to the ground floor and stepped through, unsure of what might greet her. To her surprise, at least a dozen people were in the lobby. Three of them were sleeping on chairs and the rest were huddled, talking quietly. They fell silent as Katy emerged. She turned off her flashlight and looked around.

"Uh... Hi," Katy said. "Is everything OK?" She immediately realized how silly her question sounded.

A bald-headed, red-faced man spoke in a tense voice. "Who are you? You don't look like security. You're just a kid. Security said all the upper floors were clear."

Katy's eyes narrowed for a moment, then she regained her composure. "Obviously they weren't clear. And I'm not a kid. And I work here. I was knocked out and lying on the floor up there all night long. It's too bad the security folks didn't see me."

"Well, you can't go back up. They said it's too dangerous. Off limits."

"Uh... yeah," Katy replied. This guy was really bossy, but it didn't really matter, since she didn't plan to climb back up. She looked around the group again. Everyone was still staring at her.

"What are you all doing here? Why haven't you gone home?"

"We all live out of the area," the bald man replied. "All the people who live close by left yesterday."

"And we can't get to our cars," added a plump, well-dressed woman with mascara streaks under her eyes. "It's a total mess out there, and it's dangerous. So we're waiting for the police or fire department to come help us."

Katy blinked, momentarily confused. She had just spent the last hour or so thinking about how she was going to take care of herself, and never assumed that anyone was going to help her get home.

"What makes you think the police or fire department will be able to help you?" she asked. "And where are the building security guards?"

"They left," the bald man answered. "And they told us we can't go upstairs, because it's dangerous. They said they'd get help. And don't freak everyone out with crazy questions like that. Of course someone will come to help us." He gave her a fierce look.

"When did they leave?" Katy asked.

"Last night, right after the quake. We all ran down here, and after they looked around upstairs, they came down too. They said we'd be safe in here and that we should wait."

"I don't think they're coming back," Katy replied. "And I don't think police or fire department are coming here either. I think you're on your own and should think about getting home on your own."

"They'll be here soon," the woman replied, nodding, as if trying to reassure herself.

"Yes," the man replied, again giving Katy another angry look, "they have to be on their way. And besides, what could you possibly know about it? Maybe you should just follow your own advice and leave."

"OK, suit yourself. I'm going to check out the lower level for a few minutes. I might come back this way, but will probably go out the garage exit. Good luck. By the way, if you get hungry, there are vending machines upstairs, probably on every floor.

And the building still has water pressure, at least for now. You might want to..." She looked at their blank stares. They weren't listening. "Whatever." Katy turned back toward the stairwell.

"You can't go down there," the bald man snapped. "Security said that's off-limits too. Don't even think about it."

Katy stood and looked at him for a moment, thinking about the pros and the cons of heading down the stairs. Normally she was good about following the rules, but in this case, she didn't see much sense in following a rule made by a security guard who had long ago abandoned his post. She could tell the building was relatively safe. And her focus was purely on survival, which meant making her own rules at times.

"Thanks for letting me know," Katy said, with a smile. She turned her flashlight on, opened the door, walked into the darkness.

***

Katy tested each step at first, shining her light around to look for any cracks or other signs that the stairs might collapse. The building's subterranean floors appeared to have weathered the quake well, and she picked up her pace.

Two floors down, Katy encountered her first leaky pipe. Water sprayed against the wall and ran down the stairs. She followed its path, careful to avoid slipping on the wet stairs. As she descended for another several minutes, she had visions of concrete slabs lying on crushed cars. Would she be able to find her car? Was it covered in tons of rubble?

Finally, she reached the fifth parking level. She cautiously opened the door. The beam of her flashlight penetrated the eerie blackness. Outside, there was fire, rubble, destruction, and chaos. In here, it was almost serene. She heard water dripping slowly nearby, and saw winks of light shining back at her as her flashlight's beam panned across shiny, clean cars.

The door swung shut behind her, and she took a few more, hesitant steps forward, shining her light around. There were no fallen slabs. The ceiling was intact. Aside from the darkness and the pooled water at the base of the stairwell, everything looked almost as it had when she'd parked her car yesterday morning and gone up to work.

Katy looked more closely at the exit ramp. It was completely blocked with empty cars. It appeared that many people had fled downward, despite the security guards' objections. But they clearly hadn't been able to drive anywhere.

She made her way to her Toyota Corolla and opened the front door. She sat down, pulled her cell phone from her purse, and plugged it into the 12V charging cord. The phone emitted a short beep and a small plug icon started to flash. She might as well take advantage of the car's battery now, she thought, and charge her phone. It might be a very long walk home, and there might be some kind of emergency cell service set up by now.[4]

Katy pulled the trunk release latch, got out, and took her garbage bag of supplies to the back of the car. She opened the trunk and the interior light illuminated her bright red emergency bag, nestled in the corner, next to a pair of hiking boots. She unzipped the bag, which she had configured to provide three days' worth of emergency supplies. She pulled out a light jacket and put it on. She wasn't cold anymore, but wanted to free up space to add the extra food and medical supplies she'd brought from upstairs. She inserted a water bottle into each of the two mesh side pockets, drank the last of the third bottle and dropped it in the trunk.

Next, she pulled off her pumps, put them in the trunk, and put on the lightweight boots.[5] "I'm going to miss those shoes," she thought as she laced her boots. "They were my favorites. Maybe someday I'll be back here to get them…"

She usually had a spare pair of pants and a shirt in her trunk, but two weeks earlier she'd fallen victim to a barbecue sauce spill at a friend's party. Luckily, she was able to change into clean clothes at the time. Unluckily, she hadn't gotten around to restocking her trunk. She grinned to herself for a moment, thinking about how the boots looked with her dress pants and blouse. But her appearance really didn't matter now. What mattered was the ability to keep moving.

Katy took a quick look around, more out of habit than because she was worried about anyone actually seeing her in the deserted garage. Then she opened a side panel in the trunk, which held the tire jack. It also held a small black box, about the size of a large cell phone, with two metal probes poking out of the front. She removed it from its niche in the trunk and put it in her back pocket, where it fit snugly.

Katy sat back down in the driver's seat and turned on the radio. As expected, there was no AM signal this far down in the parking garage. It usually disappeared as soon as she entered the building. But there was always the chance that FM might work. She turned the tuning knob slowly. All she could hear was static.

With a sigh, Katy pulled the charging cable from its power outlet and stashed it and her phone in her purse. She was ready to go. Purse over her shoulder, emergency bag on her back, good boots on her feet and flashlight in hand, she made her way back to the stairwell.

Because of the added weight of her pack, she ascended slowly. She opened the door marked "P-1" and stepped, blinking, into the sun-filled parking entrance. It faced east, the same direction as her home. Stowing her flashlight, she was glad she wouldn't need to make her way through the confused people waiting in the lobby above, who were probably all still huddled, right where she'd left them.

Katy's eyes were drawn to the mass of cars clogging the parking garage exit. At the intersection of the exit and the city street, several cars appeared to have crashed into each other, completely blocking the exit. They were all empty now, and they effectively trapped every other vehicle in the parking garage. She tried to remember how many people worked here. At least a couple thousand, she guessed. She wondered again about her car, and when she might be able to drive again. Just getting all of the blocking cars off of the ramps would be a time-consuming, expensive operation. And there were dozens more buildings just like it in the vicinity. What a mess.

Katy walked out to the street. The sun was over the horizon now. She welcomed the warming, bright daylight. She looked both ways before she crossed the street, and then laughed to herself. There was no traffic here, and probably wouldn't be for a long time. "Old habits die hard," she said under her breath, as she stepped over a large chunk of concrete in the middle of the street.

While this street was also clogged with cars, nothing moved and all the engines were quiet. This was apparently one of the routes people had intended to take to reach NE 8th Street, which would have taken them out of downtown, toward the suburbs. That was, until they realized there was no bridge across State Route 405, which explained why this area was so tightly packed with traffic. The street had become a car trap, just like the exit ramp in the parking garage.

About half of a block to the west, she got a better look at the collapsed building she'd seen earlier from the 27th floor. There used to be a good sandwich shop there. Now it was a smoldering pile of rubble. There were probably some bodies inside, but there was nobody on the street. She heard shouting around the corner to the west, but for whatever reason there was nobody else around here. And her home lay in the opposite direction, away from the noise.

As Katy threaded her way around rubble, heading toward the highway, she heard a helicopter in the distance, growing louder. Moments later she saw it approaching, olive green and flying low along the highway from south to north. Katy waved as it passed, but the pilot didn't see her. She was still on her own.

As the helicopter receded into the distance, the area grew strangely silent again. Where was everyone? Katy didn't see anyone on the street, on foot or in cars. When she reached the other side of the street, she looked across the highway for any signs of life. Now that she was at ground level, not up in the skyscraper anymore, she could still see columns of smoke, but couldn't see the fires that caused them. It was pretty early, she thought, but how could people still be sleeping in a situation like this?

She sat down on an abandoned car's bumper and opened her backpack. She rummaged around, pulled out a handheld radio and turned it on. It immediately beeped an alert: *"This is the emergency broadcast system. The greater Seattle area suffered a massive earthquake at 12:15 PM on Tuesday. It was centered in Seattle and measured 7.6 on the Richter scale. A state of emergency has been declared in King, Pierce, Snohomish and Kitsap counties..."* The announcement continued. It was all bad news. It sounded like most of Seattle was a disaster area, and it could be days before local residents could expect any emergency services. Katy closed her eyes and took a deep breath. She thought of the people in the lobby of her office building and shook her head. She might not be prepared for every eventuality, but she was in far better shape than they were. She stowed the radio inside her backpack and continued walking toward the highway.

Chapter 4

Neil walked at a fast pace, about four miles per hour, which wasn't bad at all, considering he'd been walking through most of the night. Since he normally enjoyed walking and hiking for exercise, this wasn't an exceptional strain on his body. The unusual part was getting only a couple of hours of sleep.

Exhausted, he'd taken a nap in an abandoned car parked on the side of the highway, a little after 2:00 A.M. Luckily, the night was cool but not cold, typical for the Pacific Northwest this time of year. He checked his watch. It was 5:45 A.M. It was still chilly, but his constant movement kept him warm.

Neil dropped his pack and sat down on a low retaining wall in front of a well-kept house. At least, it appeared to have been well-kept before the quake. Part of the wall had collapsed, dropping soil and bricks onto the sidewalk. Many of the home's windows were broken, and the roof over the porch was tilted at a precarious angle. Neil had seen far worse since the quake hit, however.

This was as good a place as any to stop. He flexed his fingers, and then rubbed his palms across his gray-flecked, day-old beard. His legs ached from the twenty miles he'd covered since the earthquake struck. He had walked all the previous afternoon and much of the night, doing his best to avoid the agitated people he encountered along the way, navigating his way past collapsed buildings and multiple fires, seeing frequent tragedy and occasional acts of heroism along the way. Despite the temptation, he hadn't stopped beyond brief pauses to rest. He was intent on reaching home and was completely focused on his goal.

This area looked safe, and for whatever reason it wasn't as damaged as other areas he'd seen as he'd passed through. Maybe it was because of the underlying geology.[6] Whatever the reason, it meant the people here were feeling relatively safe and most of them were probably still in their beds.

Neil took off his boots and peeled off his socks. He stretched out his legs, relishing the feeling of the cool air on his naked, swollen feet.[7] He reached into his backpack, pulled out an MRE, and tore it open. He wasn't very hungry, probably because he wasn't used to eating breakfast this early. But he knew he needed to eat, because he'd burned thousands of calories in the last day. If he didn't put more calories into his system soon, he'd use the last of his depleted energy reserves and start breaking down muscle for fuel. That would be bad. He could afford to burn extra fat, but not muscle. He would need the muscle later, because his trek was far from over.

First, Neil pulled out an instant coffee packet, packets of sugar and creamer, and a separate packet of hot chocolate. He tore each open and poured it into the re-sealable plastic bag that came with the MRE. He added a small amount of water from his water bottle and mashed the mixture into a smooth paste. Then he added a little more water, resealed the bag, and shook until it was thoroughly mixed. Then he filled it the rest of the way with water and shook it again. Just like a large mocha from Starbucks, he thought, as he tipped it back and took a drink. No, not quite, and there were still little undissolved chunks of something in there. It beat water though, and he needed the kick. The caffeine and sugar would quickly make its way into his system, and help keep him alert and energized. He chugged the rest.

Andrew Baze

Next, he carefully tore open the package of spaghetti with meat sauce. He hated getting the sauce on his hands, because he'd spilled it once before, and his hands smelled like the sauce for hours afterwards. This time there wouldn't be anywhere to wash his hands when he was done. He unwrapped the long-handled, plastic spoon and started eating. Halfway through, some noodles fell in his lap. He flicked them away and noticed the meat sauce stain on his pant leg. He thought back to the previous day, and how many people he'd seen with bloodstained clothing or bandages. He was lucky. This was only sauce.

Chapter 5

Now that Katy was farther away from downtown and it's signal-blocking, high-rise buildings, she took out her handheld amateur radio[8] and turned the channel selector to "EMRGNCY-N", her neighborhood's emergency, simplex[9] frequency on the two-meter ham radio band.

"This is Katy, KE5HTI. Can anyone hear me? I'm trying to reach Jeff Parker or anyone else in my neighborhood. Please come in."

The radio was silent. She tried again. There was still no reply. Then she remembered. She dropped her backpack, opened it up and pulled out a quart-sized, plastic freezer bag. It held her spare batteries, extra "stubby" antenna[10], and Nifty Guide.[11] She fished around and pulled out a piece of paper covered with names, phone numbers, times and frequencies. It was her calling clock.[12]

In addition to the telephone contact information for friends and relatives in and out of the area, the calling clock contained the following information.

Plan D	Method	2M Handheld radio
	Who	Jeff and neighbors
	When	Every hour on the hour, for ten minutes (until nn:10). If power is <50%, only call on even hours. Transmit every five minutes; monitor the rest of the time. (Between midnight and 5:00 AM, probably wasting batteries.)
	Frequency	**146.660 MHz**. If it's busy, try **147.660**. If that's busy, try **147.550**.
	Notes	NA

Figure 1. Excerpt from Katy's calling clock, a key part of an emergency communication plan.

Just one month earlier, Katy had opened an email to find an updated file from her neighbor Jeff Parker, which contained new phone numbers for some people who had just moved into a rental down the street. Unfortunately, she hadn't updated her radio with the new neighborhood emergency frequencies. While she was generally pretty organized, she wasn't a fanatic about always updating all of the details. But she did remember to print out the document and stuff it in the emergency bag. After a couple of attempts, referring once to the Nifty Guide, Katy was able to update the frequency in her radio[13] and store it in memory. She transmitted again.

"This is Katy, KE5HTI. Can anyone hear me? I'm headed home on foot and will be actively monitoring for another five minutes. Then I'll switch to the calling clock and transmit every hour on the hour." There was still no reply.

Katy bent the flexible antenna[14] almost in half and slipped the radio into her purse. Then she picked up her backpack, zipped it

28

shut and put it on. It was time to start walking home. Hopefully my home is still standing, she thought.

She walked south, toward where the street descended closer to the level of the highway. She only had about five miles to walk, almost directly east, which would take less than two hours on a normal day. But today was not a normal day. Nonetheless, she would still ideally be home by this afternoon.

After about twenty yards, she reached the street that ran parallel to the highway. She followed it until she saw that the gravel slope that led down to the highway had become less steep. She carefully made her way down the bank, slipping a couple times, but staying on her feet. When she reached the bottom, she hopped over the narrow, water-filled drainage ditch and walked up the short slope on the far side and onto the highway.

As she stepped from the gravel area to the concrete, she stumbled and caught herself by grabbing onto the side of a green Chevy Suburban parked on the shoulder. She jumped and almost screamed when she saw a head pop up on the driver's side. Katy stopped in her tracks and stared at the driver. The driver stared back with bleary eyes. Then Katy regained her composure and gently knocked on the window. The woman turned the key in the ignition and powered the window down. It moved very slowly. The battery was probably close to being dead. Katy looked at her curiously.

"Are you OK?" Katy asked.

"Yes. Can you help me?" the woman asked.

"What are you doing here?"

"I couldn't drive anymore. The road is blocked. I live in Marysville. There is no way I'll be able to walk that far. I was hoping the National Guard would come by today to help me get home. I ran out of gas, because it was cold last night and I needed the heater…"

Katy looked at her sympathetically.

"Yeah, it was cold. I was lying on the floor next to a broken window all night," Katy said. Then she shook her head gently as she delivered the bad news. "I wouldn't count on the National Guard showing up anytime soon. The traffic jam behind you probably extends for miles. In the meantime, you might be better off taking shelter in a building downtown. There are people up there," Katy said as she pointed to the nearby, mostly intact high-rises. "Some of the buildings are wrecked, but some of them are newer and still standing. And there is probably still some food and water. At least some water. And probably a toilet."

The woman looked embarrassed. "Yeah... Last night I had to..." She glanced over at the jagged remains of the bridge that jutted out several feet over the highway.

"I know there are people in that bank building right there." Katy pointed to her building. "In the lobby. They're waiting too."

"I don't know if I can climb up that slope," the woman said apprehensively.

"You'll find a way." Katy turned to continue her walk home.

"I *am* thirsty..." The woman stared at Katy's water bottle poking out of her backpack's side pocket. "Can I have that water?"

"There should still be plenty of water in any of those buildings up there." Katy was reluctant to share her meager resources, since she had no idea what lay between here and home. "Good luck."

"But... Hey, can't you help me?" the woman demanded. Her tone had changed from pitiful to indignant. Katy continued walking away.

A second later, Katy heard a horn honk briefly, and turned back to see the woman's head on the steering wheel. She appeared to be crying. Katy scowled with frustration, but couldn't resist. She walked back to the SUV and knocked on the partially opened window again. The woman didn't look up.

"You can make it up there just fine. You'll be OK. Come on!"

The woman looked up. "I'm so worried about my family. I have two little girls," she sobbed.

"I understand. But you need to take care of yourself right now. They're probably fine. Marysville is far away from here and may not even be damaged. You need to find shelter, water and food until help comes. Let's go. Get out and go."

Katy reached out and opened the driver's side door. The woman stepped out and wiped her eyes with her sleeve. She carried nothing but a small, bright pink wallet.

"Do you have a three-day bag or a car emergency kit?" Katy asked. The woman looked at her blankly. "How about a first aid kit in the glove box? Some snacks in the back somewhere? Any emergency supplies at all?"

"No."

Katy paused. There was no reason to discourage the woman further by being critical. Then she took a deep breath, exhaled and willed herself to smile at the lady. "Then off you go!" She pointed up the gentle embankment. "You'll be OK. Get up there. Your family will be OK and so will you. I have to go now."

"Can I come with you?"

Katy looked her up and down, noting the rhinestone-studded flip-flops at the bottom of sausage-like legs protruding from her short skirt.

"Can you walk five miles over rough ground?" she asked. The woman scowled.

"You can help me."

Katy shook her head.

"I don't think so. You'd be better off just trying to reach one of these nearby buildings and waiting with the others. Besides," she added, tipping her head eastward, "I know you're not going to want to walk through that neighborhood. That's where I'm headed."

Katy didn't wait around to talk with the woman any longer. There was no point. She already did what she could, and she could only help so much. She ignored the woman's cries of indignation and went on her way.

When Katy reached the Jersey barrier at the center of the highway, she climbed up and looked down the highway at the traffic jam. The earlier honk of the woman's horn apparently woke some people up. She counted at least a dozen faces, some in pairs, sitting in some of the intact vehicles, waiting for someone to come and rescue them. As she watched, she saw that some of them looked over and noticed the woman scrambling up the embankment in her flip-flops. A couple of doors opened and people got out to get a better look. Maybe the woman would inspire them, Kate thought, as she turned and hopped off the barrier. She didn't look back.

Katy jogged across the northbound lanes and made her way up the embankment, to the on-ramp, and onto NE 8th Street. She had crossed I-405, a step in the right direction. There were no more bridges between here and home.

Remembering that she had left her radio on in case someone was trying to return her earlier call, she reached into her purse and turned it off. Nobody appeared to be on the air at the moment, at least on this frequency. Then Katy looked to the east, and her eyes narrowed.

Chapter 6

Rodney and Jimmy woke up unusually early, which was any time before 10:00 A.M. Their mother's bellowing was worse than any alarm clock.

"Get out of bed! There's free stuff at the Ace Hardware!"

Jimmy turned over and opened his eyes from the other side of the room, and looked at the massive, round silhouette in the doorway.

"I said get up, you lazy dirtbags," she yelled again. "Go get us some stuff before it's all gone. Everyone is coming back with tons of good stuff. We need some stuff too!"

"Free stuff," Jimmy mumbled. "Cool." Groaning, he sat up and swung his legs out of bed, as his mother shuffled off.

From his bed on the opposite side of the room, Rodney did the same. "Yeah, let's get us some stuff." His bleary eyes suddenly brightened and blinked rapidly. "Hey, what about the liquor store?" He grinned at Jimmy, who grinned back. They grabbed yesterday's clothes from the floor and began yanking them back on.

"Mom!" Rodney shouted as he walked out of the bedroom. "What's for breakfast?"

"Idiot!" she shouted. "We ain't got no power, so I can't cook. And the fridge is stinky already, 'cause you dummies opened it too many times last night. Now get your lazy butts outside and get us some food."

"Jeez," Jimmy whined, as they shuffled to the door. "Can't even have breakfast!"

"Yeah, we can," Rodney whispered, elbowing him and grinning. "At the liquor store. Whatever Ma wants at the hardware store can wait."

"I bet she wants a flashlight and batteries," Jimmy said, looking around the darkened house.

"Whatever. We got priorities."

They stepped out of the building and stopped on the sidewalk.

"Whoa," Rodney said. "Look at that." He pointed across the street. "They are screwed."

The much older, brick apartment building directly across from theirs had partly collapsed, and a portion of the front wall had fallen away completely, exposing the interiors of several apartments. The sidewalk in front of the building was piled high with bricks and other debris, and two grime-coated men were moving bricks to the side. They looked exhausted. One of them called halfheartedly "Shawna? Kelly? Can you hear me?" There was no reply.

"We ain't got time to mess with this – we need stuff," Jimmy said, after a few seconds of staring. The destruction was interesting, but they had places to go.

They moved quickly now as visions of long, sparkling rows of liquor bottles danced in their heads. They were only three blocks away.

A few minutes later, as they crossed the street not far from the liquor store, they noticed the acrid smell of smoke. This wasn't pleasant-smelling smoke like from a barbecue. This smoke was full of stink, fumes from burning rubber, wood, cloth, and other substances that weren't supposed to be burned. They walked faster, eager to see what was happening. This was a lot better than TV.

Jimmy and Rodney turned the corner and gaped. The "stop and rob" mini-mart on the corner was completely engulfed in flames. Three men stood outside, laughing. One of them picked up a small chunk of broken concrete from the rubble and threw it through the last unbroken window. It shattered and flames shot out.

"Oh yeah!" one of them shouted. "He's been ripping us off for years. Finally got his. That's what you get for charging six bucks a pack for cigarettes!"

The others laughed, then started looking around for other things to throw, break, or burn, already bored by this burning building.

Jimmy and Rodney looked at each other, wondering the same thing. Was the liquor store still in one piece? They broke into a jog, crossing the street and moving up the block, away from the arsonists.

The sign was still there. "Tim's Liquor and Wine." But the flashing, buzzing light in the faded plastic sign wasn't lit and the glass panels on the front doors were all broken.

They entered the store and both scowled simultaneously. Almost every shelf was empty and the floor was littered with broken glass and slick with a mixture of spilled alcohol. The air was thick with fumes and their eyes were already watering, but they had a mission and weren't going to be deterred.

"Come on," Rodney said. "There has to be something left." He walked to a back shelf where one bottle still stood, lonely on the shelf. "Apricot schnapps," muttered with disgust. But he grabbed it anyway. "Where's the Jack Daniels?"

"No way there's any of that left," Jimmy said. "But here's something interesting. Get over here."

"What's up? There has to be something left over here. Give me a sec." Rodney called from the other side of the store.

"Not as good as this," Jimmy called back.

Rodney cursed and crunched over in the broken glass, then slipped in a puddle of wine and almost fell down. "If I get hurt in here I'm gonna sue someone for making a hazardous environment," he said resolutely. Then he saw what Jimmy was looking at. "Whoa!"

"Yeah," Jimmy replied. "The same guy that called the cops on us last year." He stepped toward the man who sat, propped against the wall. The man's face was bloody and his was nose swollen, and he cradled an injured arm close to his body. His eyes were slits. He appeared to be on the edge of consciousness.

"Hey man," Rodney demanded, "where's the cash box? And where's the rest of the booze?"

The man didn't move. Rodney kicked his outstretched leg. The man's eyes slowly opened the rest of the way, and his gaze fell on the two men.

"All gone," he said in a raspy whisper, mouth barely opening. "They took it."

"No way," Rodney said. "There's more, and you're holding out on us." He delivered a sharp kick to the man's thigh. "Do you want to get beat some more? Tell us where you hide stuff!"

The man didn't say a word. Rodney kicked him again, harder. The man grunted in pain as Rodney's foot connected with his tender ribs.

"He ain't got nothin' left. Someone else already beat it out of him," Jimmy said. "But this is for calling the cops on us last year," he said as he delivered a kick of his own. He was rewarded with a groan, as the man toppled over and curled into the fetal position.

"You're lucky we don't torch this place with you in it," Jimmy shouted over his shoulder as he walked out. He looked at Rodney. "Let's go find a lighter, too. Maybe we'll need to burn something down later," he said, and they laughed.

Chapter 7

Neil walked along the highway. Even after what he'd seen so far, he was amazed by what he saw now. He stopped. From his current position, he could see dozens of columns of smoke rising over Seattle. To the north, in Bellevue, he could see two ominously large columns of smoke. Although much of the construction on the East Side was newer than in Seattle, it obviously hadn't been spared the effects of the massive quake.

He looked at Seattle again, and in addition to the smoke, he could make out two large helicopters hovering over the city. One of them dropped a large load of water onto something out of view. "You don't see that every day," he thought to himself. The helicopter was attempting to put out a fire the way they often put out fires in the wilderness, where fire trucks couldn't get access. With just a few seconds of violent shaking, over a hundred years of industrious effort had been transformed into a virtual, concrete wilderness.

Neil's thoughts returned to his wife, Renee. She hadn't answered any of his radio calls. This wasn't a big surprise, because he was still far away from the house, and the propagation tests[15] they'd conducted last year indicated he'd be lucky if a signal reached home from this area, but it didn't stop him from trying frequently. In fact, he didn't really expect to be able to reach Renee until getting north of downtown Bellevue, which would take at least another couple of hours.

For an instant, he allowed negative thoughts to intrude, and imagined her pinned underneath a pile of rubble, weakly crying out his name. He took a deep breath and cleared his head. He had no reason to think she was in any danger. Their house was relatively new, and they knew their neighbors pretty well. She had to be OK.

In a perfect post-earthquake world, he would be talking with Renee effortlessly, using a different radio. He thought about the one he left back in his truck. It was an inexpensive, small, low-power, high-frequency radio that could only transmit Morse code. He kept it with him just for fun, and once in a while, usually when he was driving up in the mountains, he'd take the opportunity to stop, string out the 120-foot dipole [16] antenna somewhere convenient, call "CQ," [17] and listen for any other hams in the area. To keep it convenient, he would set up the antenna close to the ground, transmitting with the "NVIS" – Near Vertical Incidence Skywave [18] method, which allowed him to chat with other hams at a distance of up to approximately 400 miles.

The day before, after running outside with the rest of his coworkers, Neil immediately went to his truck and retrieved his get-home bag, which contained that radio. As he hurriedly reorganized the contents, Neil removed the HF radio, its spare batteries and several other items, to save weight. Each time he came to an item that he wasn't sure he'd need, he reminded himself of the backpacking trip he'd taken several years earlier, a trip that taught him a valuable lesson. When he had filled his backpack for that trip, he'd streamlined ruthlessly, taking the least weight possible. His friend, on the other hand, had brought extras of almost everything. While they were both in excellent condition and usually competitive with their pace while hiking, his friend had been exhausted at the end of the second long day of hiking, but Neil still had a lot of energy left. It taught him that weight may not be an issue initially, but it eventually took its toll. So in this case, Neil took the same approach, packing only what was absolutely necessary.

The fact that Renee wouldn't be listening on HF anyway made his decision easier. Getting her to practice for a few minutes with the small VHF handheld radio was a challenge all by itself. And she had actually been far more patient and understanding than most of his ham buddies' wives, so he counted his blessings and didn't push it. The handheld radio was the only realistic solution for them in a situation like this.

Neil's top priority was speed. Yes, maybe someone would loot the leftover gear from his truck, and maybe not. He'd find out eventually. But at this point, the other radio and other gear didn't matter nearly as much as getting home fast, so he wasn't going to lose sleep over it.

Neil changed the channel on his handheld Icom radio to the government's emergency alert frequency. The same recorded message he'd heard all night was still playing. There was no new news.

If he made good time, he'd be home before nightfall, in Renee's arms. When he knew she was safe, the rest of the world and its problems wouldn't matter so much.

Chapter 8

"Mama's gonna be pissed," Jimmy said matter-of-factly, then took another swig from the half-empty bottle. The apricot schnapps, sweet and a thick, was the only liquor they'd found. They spent the last hour combing the area, looking in any stores they could find for electronics, tools, batteries, alcohol, and even food. But many other people in the neighborhood were the early birds, stripping all shelves in the area bare. Rodney and Jimmy were left with nothing more than a bottle of apricot schnapps and a few Slim Jims they'd found on the floor of another devastated mini-mart. Jimmy passed the bottle to Rodney.

"What's left?" Rodney asked, then took a gulp. It hadn't tasted good earlier, and it didn't taste good now. But it dulled his senses a little, and in this chaos, that felt like a good thing. "Mama's gonna expect us to come home with somethin'. Everyone else is comin' home with stuff, and if we come home with a half-empty bottle, we're dead meat. At least some cigarettes and a flashlight or somethin'."

"There's the grocery store down on 140th," Jimmy said. "Lots of rich folks shop down there, so they're probably linin' up and payin' for stuff. We could probably take whatever we want and just run out."

"They got cigarettes?"

"Sure. And booze. Better than this." Jimmy took another gulp, made a face, and handed the bottle to Rodney.

"Nah, it'll take too long to walk down there. The longer we take, the more pissed Mama's gonna be."

"What else we gonna do?"

"We could take other people's stuff. Let's find someone alone. Two against one. We take his stuff and bring it home."

"Hmm." He took another gulp. "You're smart."

"Oh yeah. I'm a genius. Let's go find someone," Rodney replied with a grin.

From their walk earlier that morning, Rodney and Jimmy had a good idea which roads were being used most. Like ants following a pheromone trail back and forth from a dead bird to their nest, many people were returning from the businesses in the area, bringing what was left of the merchandise back to their apartments, and the more industrious of the looters were heading back out for more. But not everyone followed the main roads, and that's what Rodney and Jimmy were counting on.

Lying in wait behind a parked car, on a road parallel to the main ant trail in this area, they waited for a single person to come by, carrying something they wanted. And now someone was approaching.

A lone boy who looked about fifteen years old was approaching at a healthy pace, considering his size compared to the weight of the heavy milk crate he was carrying. His eyes widened in surprise as Jimmy stepped out from behind the car, blocking his path. The boy glanced over his shoulder, and saw Rodney coming up behind him, blocking his retreat.

"Don't move," Jimmy hissed, pointing his knife at the boy, the shiny blade glinting in the sunlight.

The boy stood, not moving muscle, eyes riveted on the knife.

"Where'd you get the stuff?" Jimmy demanded.

"You can have it." He bent over quickly and set it down.

"Don't move!" Jimmy hissed again.

"I got it at the store on 140th" the boy said, a tremor in his voice.

41

"How'd you get it without getting caught?"

"I went in the back. They had these crates there, and there was still lots of stuff in the storage area."

"Get lost," Rodney said, delivering a forceful slap to the back of the boy's head. The boy pitched forward, almost tripping over the crate. Without another word he bolted across the street and back the way he'd come.

"OK," Jimmy said, as he put his knife back in its sheath. "Now we got stuff. Let's give it to Mama and then find someone else. But even if that store had stuff left, why should we walk all the way down there to get it? Someone else will do the work for us. We'll just hang out around here and collect it."

"Take it up to Mama. I'll keep an eye out for other good stuff," Rodney said.

"You do it."

"No, you do it."

"I have the knife," Jimmy said. "I'm in charge."

Rodney looked at Jimmy. His brother was just crazy enough to use the knife if someone pushed him. "Fine. Be right back."

Chapter 9

Katy stood on the sidewalk that paralleled NE 8th, eying its path as it travelled uphill and eastward. From this lower angle she couldn't see farther than the next 150 yards, at which point the road levelled out and then dipped out of sight. She dreaded what she would see when she got that far.

She had travelled about three quarters of a mile eastward from downtown Bellevue, past lightly damaged buildings, many with small groups of people already working on clearing away broken glass and rubble. Curiously, there was no looting going on, and she didn't understand why. It made her feel a little safer, but the feeling of safety diminished with each step she took toward North Lake, the only bad neighborhood in this part of the city.

During the day, travelling on NE 8th in North Lake was usually no problem. It was regularly patrolled by Bellevue Police Department cruisers, usually with two officers at a time. There was minor gang activity, but the neighborhood itself was a generally disorganized threat, either because there weren't enough businesses to extort or because the police kept a lid on other activities that enabled gangs to bring in cash. But it was still not a safe place to travel on foot.

At night, it was patrolled, but not as well. Most people who knew the area didn't go there at night, because they knew the locals took to the streets, usually on side streets where the police travelled less frequently. Sometimes, people from out of the area ventured down these roads after dark, usually in search of drugs, and the less savvy were frequently mugged or worse.

Unfortunately, this neighborhood lay between Katy and her home. Driving was not an option now, and neither was walking around it. Katy had done her research. Aside from the extra miles it would add to her travel, she knew that the best alternate route would require crossing another bridge, one much older than the collapsed overpass she'd just skirted. There was no way it would be safe to cross, even if it were still standing. And that bridge didn't have gentle embankments on either side. It could take her hours just to get around that area and back on track, assuming the route was passable at all. She would have to go through North Lake.

Katy breathed heavily as she crested the hill. She was making good time while she could. This was the first of many hills between the downtown area and her neighborhood, which lay almost directly east. She slowed her pace and walked over toward the small strip mall parking lot that spanned the top of the hill on the right side of the road. She walked up to the large, one-story building as she moved farther east. It was an unusual way for a pedestrian to travel, but this was not a common situation, and she needed to be discreet. She knew that she'd be less of a potential target if she avoided the sidewalks. As she reached the end of the building, her view eastward improved and she was able to see down into the small valley ahead.

Katy dug around in her backpack and pulled a small pair of binoculars. She'd always wondered whether she'd ever need them, but since they didn't weigh much or take up a lot of space, and she didn't have anywhere better to store them, she kept them in her emergency bag. Now she was grateful she had them. "Be prepared" was more than the Girl Scouts' motto, which she'd taken to naturally many years earlier; it was part of her personality. Whether it was because her parents had raised her with that mentality or because she had been wired that way from birth, she didn't know, but the result in this case was this handy pair of binoculars, ready to use.

Katy leaned against the wall to steady the binoculars and gazed down NE 8th into the small valley. About a mile away, she saw what she'd feared and expected. A group of young men stood behind a car parked sideways in the middle of the street. On the near side of the improvised roadblock, three more cars and a truck sat empty, doors open.

She scanned to the right. On the south side of the road, where business owners tried to make a living tucked behind bars or bullet-proof Plexiglas barriers, most of the storefronts had gaping, jagged holes where their windows used to be. Looters had probably broken out most of the windows spared by the earthquake.

Only a few people moved in or out of the buildings. They weren't running excitedly, and they didn't have much in their arms. She saw one man carrying a metal shelf, and another following him, staggering with what looked like a very heavy cash register. The register was probably empty, as the looter would learn when he finally beat it open. Maybe there was nothing else left to loot in this area.

She tore her eyes away from what she usually would have considered fascinating TV footage. Katy recalled the endless video footage broadcast after Hurricane Katrina. Since New Orleans was so far away, the rioting and looting she saw never quite felt real. And she never expected to see it where she lived.

What was interesting on video was terrifying in person. And with this new reality came a whole new set of rules. Katy knew that if she didn't learn and follow them quickly, she would be in real danger.

Now Katy wished she had her gun. Better yet, she wanted two guns, a good combat rifle or shotgun, with her handgun for backup. Even if most societal rules went out the window, she could still enforce her very favorite rule: "Don't hurt or kill

Katy." A gun would really encourage people to follow that rule. But now she'd have to find another way. She'd have to get by on her wits.

Katy scanned further east, pausing briefly to observe a fight. Two men were on the ground next to a partially collapsed taco shack, grappling and occasionally punching each other. But the tide turned in an instant when a third man appeared and kicked one of the men three times, hard. This fight was over. It was ugly. Katy looked away. "I don't need to see this," she thought. A moment later, she heard a scream, in a different direction. Someone else was in trouble.

Katy knew she would have to take a different road. This main stretch was clearly off-limits to a woman travelling alone. Some of the people down there were probably armed with knives or guns. It was starting to look like a war zone.

Then it struck her. Why weren't people coming downtown to loot? It didn't make sense. There were so many upscale stores downtown, all containing expensive merchandise which was certainly worth looting. Katy continued scanning with the binoculars, tracking the road back from the middle of the valley, scanning closer and closer to her current location until she saw it. A wide chasm crossed the roadway, extending into the wooded area on the left and behind a small business on the right. Too broad to jump, it acted as an effective, natural roadblock. Katy panned back toward her location. She'd somehow missed it earlier. On her side of the massive fissure sat a police car. She couldn't tell whether it had any officers inside, but one thing was clear. None of the locals were travelling westward on NE 8th Street.

Katy spotted the body of a man lying not far from the police car, in a dark puddle that was most likely blood. He lay face down, unmoving. And judging by the contorted position he was in, there was no way he was taking a nap. Maybe he had threatened a police officer. It appeared that the combination of a dead man, a wide crevasse in the road, and a police car on the other side acted as an effective deterrent to anyone thinking of going west.

Someone would eventually find a way around this obstacle, as the lure of the expensive downtown businesses would be too strong to resist. But for now, it appeared that the downtown area was safe from the looters.

None of this helped Katy, though. She needed to travel east, and the police car in this part of the neighborhood wouldn't do her any good, unless an officer was willing to loan her a shotgun. That wouldn't happen, she thought with a wry smile. In fact, if any police saw her, they would probably try to stop her from continuing eastward.

She kept her eyes pressed to the binoculars, looking for another option. Several drab, hulking apartment buildings squatted on the south side of NE 8th Street. They were probably trouble. She would have to travel far out of her way to circumvent them and pass through the less dangerous neighborhood to the south. On the north side of the road were several homes and dead-end streets, but she could also see a greenbelt and some tall power line towers.

Katy hadn't paid much attention to the towers before. They weren't very visible from the road, but she remembered someone telling her they were the main reason for the greenbelt. The center of the greenbelt was the path for the massive power lines carrying high-voltage current from a regional power substation toward the city center. If these towers were like the ones she'd run along while training for cross-country in high school, there would be an open road near the lines, used for inspection and maintenance.

But the greenbelt was to the north of 8th, and her home was farther to the south. Going north would take quite a bit longer, and more than anything she wanted to get home as quickly as possible. Feeling impatient, Katy decided to head south.

It looked like the best choice at the time.

Chapter 10

"Dad, we have three more people who need help, on 38th Street. They have cuts and scrapes, and maybe a broken foot, but nothing serious. The house number is 1349."

Jeff jotted it down in his notebook and made a call on his handheld FRS/GMRS radio[19].

"Mark, we have three more yellows at 1348 38th Street."

"Got it," Jeff's radio chirped in reply. "Three yellows at 1348 38th."

"That's two blacks, seven reds, eighteen yellows, and the rest green so far," Jeff said, counting from his notebook.

The CERT[20] system used colors to triage people for medical treatment. The two people treated as "black" were dead, a husband and wife whose house had collapsed on them. There could be more fatalities, but it would take time to find them in the rubble. Searching in and around collapsed buildings was dangerous, and lower priority than helping others who needed urgent care. The top priority now was to treat people who needed medical attention most, the ones assessed as "reds." [21]

"The two reds at 1219 36th are stabilized," Matt's voice said, over the radio.

Jeff made another note in his notebook. He looked over at the map.

"The next closest is the one on 13th Place. That's your next stop." He paused. "How are you and Paula doing? Are you

49

staying hydrated? Do you still have enough supplies? Do you need anything else?"

Robbie listened closely. Many times that morning he'd jumped on his bike with a backpack full of supplies and ridden as fast as he could to where Mark and Paula, their neighborhood medical team, had been helping injured neighbors. In addition to working with his father, who was operating radios to communicate with different teams in the neighborhood, Robbie was tasked as a runner, to ride around the neighborhood, distributing critical, time-sensitive supplies.

"We're OK for now," Mark replied.

Robbie's radio chirped again.

"Search team checking in. We checked out the collapsed house at 1218 40th. We can't hear anyone. No signs of life."

"Got it, Pavel, thanks," Robbie said. He walked to the map on the wall and made a mark. "I don't know how we would do this without a map," he told Jeff. "It would be hard to keep track."

"Yeah," Jeff replied. "It's a good thing we printed it before we had an emergency. We'd have a hard time finding online maps with no Internet connection." He looked over at the map of the neighborhood. Before today, it had been a small stack of paper sitting in a file folder, which he collected several months ago when he ran a "Map Your Neighborhood" program[22] with his neighbors. Now, it was taped up on the wall and both he and Robbie had been marking it up and sticking post-its on it throughout the morning. It helped them get a "big picture" view of the surrounding neighborhood.

"Oh yeah," Robbie said, thinking about the power supply, "I almost forgot. How long do we need to run the generator?"

"Thanks for the reminder. We should probably shut it off for now and conserve gas."

All morning they had been running the generator, mostly to lower the refrigerator temperature back to normal, and to keep their radios charged. In addition, they had plugged in almost everything they owned that used a rechargeable battery, and hooked up their two deep-cycle, 12-volt batteries to chargers. While they were conscientious about plugging different things in at certain times, in order to make best use of the generator's power output, they benefitted from the generator's power output regulator. It was an inverter generator, engineered with an economy mode that allowed it to slow down when less power was required, which saved fuel. Relatively little of the power produced by the generator had gone to waste[23]. And now that everything was fully charged, they could shut it off for a while.

"I'll do it," Robbie offered. He clipped his radio to his belt and walked out of the room and down the stairs. Moments later, he stood in front of the generator, which was humming efficiently. He reached down and turned the main switch to the "Off" position. It quickly sputtered to a stop.

He walked back into the kitchen, where his mother was turning off the butane stove. She looked over her shoulder. "Time for second breakfast. Go tell your dad."

Robbie walked back to the office, where he found Jeff making more notations on the map.

"Good news," Jeff said. "All in all, it's not as bad as we thought. Most of the neighborhood is OK, and only a few houses are seriously damaged. If the darn roads weren't so messed up, we'd be even better off. I'll bet there are a lot of people who want to come back home, but they can't drive."

Throughout the morning, in addition to tracking his neighbors' health status, Jeff had also been mapping blocked roads. So far, it appeared that their neighborhood was effectively blocked at some point in every direction. Aside from a hole in the fence along I-90, which Jeff himself had cut when coming home the previous day, they were blocked to the south too. If it wasn't a fallen tree or power line, it was a pile of abandoned cars and trucks.

"Mom says it's time to eat again. You have to keep your energy up," Robbie said, interrupting Jeff's thoughts.

"Can you bring it in here for me?" Jeff asked. "It's still pretty crazy out there, and I need to stay close to the radio. Someone else might need me."

Chapter 11

Katy walked down the sidewalk, parallel to the massive fissure. She occasionally glanced down, still amazed at its depth. Sometimes she'd see protruding, broken pipes or torn cables, or things that had fallen from the street level. Just a minute earlier she'd walked closer to the edge and seen three cars that had fallen and wedged themselves in, about fifteen feet below street level. She hoped nobody was trapped inside. After that eye-opening view, she kept her distance from the edge.

At one point, the fissure veered toward a building, or what remained of a building. Katy could see one wall still standing on the far side, but most of it had disappeared. She remembered seeing pictures of a giant sinkhole that had opened up under a house in Florida the year before. It looked something like this. But this felt a lot worse.

The crack wasn't straight, though it generally meandered southward, and luckily for most of the people in the area, it seemed to generally split the roadway, instead of swallowing all of the buildings.

Next to the sidewalk that Katy followed, tall buildings loomed. The landscape had changed again. Now she was in "the projects." The neighborhood's drab colors added to the gloomy mood, and the occasional scowling face in a window didn't help either. As she passed close to one building, she saw several large cracks in the exterior. She didn't know anything about evaluating a building for safety after an earthquake, but it didn't take a genius to see this one wasn't safe. She was surprised it hadn't collapsed yet.

Katy tried to imagine what they were like inside. Even though these apartment buildings were still upright, the quake's force must have caused many new problems. Aside from exterior issues such as cracks and masonry falling off in some places, there must have been damage to plumbing and electrical wiring. Regardless, these people wouldn't have elevators, electricity, light, water or flushing toilets. It would only take a day or two for the conditions inside to get even worse than their normal, substandard levels. These people would be living in medieval conditions in no time.

She remembered her neighbor Jeff talking about a U.S. Geological Survey website that showed the underlying geology by neighborhood, but she never got around to looking at it herself. Weaving around piles of rubble and tipped-over garbage cans, she wondered whether her own house and neighborhood had been flattened or left standing. Regardless, she had to get home, and she would figure out what to do from there.

Katy heard a window opening above her.

"Hey! When does the power and water come back?" a woman shouted down from the third floor.

"I don't know. I'm just passing through," Katy shouted back.

"Where are you going? To the shelter? Where is it? We need lunch," the woman barked.

"I don't know where any shelters are," Katy said, growing uncomfortable. She didn't feel like having a shouting conversation with this woman. She didn't want any attention in this neighborhood.

"What the heck good are you then!" the woman shouted back angrily. The window slammed shut.

Katy sighed with relief and started walking again. For the people trapped in their homes with no power for their televisions, any news was good news, but Katy had none to offer.

The question did make her want to check her radio again. But the last thing she wanted to do now was to pull out her radio and listen for an update. She'd either be surrounded by people wanting to listen in, or someone would yank it out of her hands and run away. All she wanted to do was get out of there.

Picking up her pace, Katy crossed the next intersection and got a better view of the fissure as it stretched ahead of her. In the distance, she saw it narrow. She looked more closely. A little farther, it ended. That was the way out.

But she saw more than the end of the chasm. She saw a lot of people crossing in this area. There must a department store not far from here, she thought, because she saw several men with armloads of clothes, another carrying a microwave oven and two more carrying flat-panel televisions, the pictures on their boxes advertising their contents in bright colors. The area had become a main thoroughfare, and foot traffic was increasing as other locals saw the goods their neighbors were hauling away. Everyone seemed to follow a general path from their neighborhood to a nearby shopping area.

The looting wasn't shocking any more. So many things could change in a day. Unlike in Japan after the devastating earthquake and tsunami of early 2011, which resulted in the survivors waiting in orderly lines and generally respecting others' property, it appeared that many of Bellevue's residents saw the absence of law enforcement and other government structures as an opportunity to "get rich," that is, if one defined being rich as owning a large screen TV or a new microwave. Katy watched as she walked, trying from a distance to feel the energy of the crowd. As long as they were focused on taking other people's stuff versus getting in her way, she suspected she might be safe.

As she got closer to the unbroken ground, her excitement grew. This was another step closer to home. She could just walk to the east like everyone else and be on her way. But then she slowed down, cautioning herself. This was no time to let her guard down.

Katy stopped and sat on the sidewalk near a parked car. She pulled out her binoculars and took a closer look at the intersection. She was still far enough away to not be noticeable by the people ahead, but could now get a much better idea of what it would be like to cross. She waited patiently and watched.

Katy frowned. Some industrious thugs had set up shop in the middle of the road and were casually watching the steady stream of looters. As she watched, one of the men, pointing a handgun, walked up to one of the looters. After a few seconds of shouting, the looter directed the man to a nearby house. A minute later the man came out with empty hands and a scowl on his face. He went back the way he'd come, probably planning to recoup his losses.

"That's a smart way to do it," Katy said to herself. "Let the others do the work for you. And nobody can complain about getting robbed, since they're all robbing someone else in the first place."

This was a serious problem. While Katy saw a few women walking together with men, she didn't see any women walking alone. And to complicate matters, Katy definitely didn't fit in with the locals. Aside from her boots, her clothes were nicer and more conservative than those the other women were wearing. She also didn't walk or talk the way they did. To top it off, she was carrying a bright red backpack. The color would be helpful if someone was trying to find her in the woods, but it was definitely the wrong color if she was trying to blend in. Katy quietly growled in frustration. This wouldn't work. She had to take a different route.

Katy cursed under her breath, packed her binoculars and turned back the way she'd come.

The south side of the fissure was a danger zone. Heading north was the only other option, unless she wanted to take up residence somewhere downtown and wait for help that would probably be a long time coming.

Frustrated, she backtracked, crossed NE 8th again, and continued north, hoping to find the far end of the fissure without wasting too much time. She passed where she had started earlier and kept going, determined to find a way around.

After about a quarter mile, the fissure ended in the middle of the block. She would be able to head east again at the next intersection. The area was zoned for business, and was populated with doctors' offices, a preschool, some law offices, but nothing of particular interest to looters, it seemed. The streets here were quiet, and the occasional people she passed on the sidewalk ignored her.

Playing it safe, Katy walked one block farther, well past the end of the fissure, before crossing to the east.

She walked parallel to the greenbelt she'd observed earlier, and after few minutes she approached a low, locked gate that provided vehicle access to the power company. On either side of the gate stood large patches of blackberry bushes. The gate wasn't a problem though. The metal bar, designed to keep out cars, was no obstacle for someone on foot. She easily stepped over it.

About twenty yards down the dirt road, Katy looked up at one of the massive towers. It stood straight up, seemingly unaffected by the massive quake. The thick cables were another story. About fifty yards ahead, a section of wire had snapped and lay on the ground. Katy kept her distance. The access road ran alongside the path of the power lines, not directly underneath. She doubted the lines still carried power, but the only way to find out was to risk her life by getting close, and there was no way she'd do that.

The grass near the dirt and gravel path appeared to have been mowed recently, so the path was unobstructed and relatively straight, definitely easier and safer than the streets. She would eventually have to leave this road and go into another neighborhood, but for now it was smooth sailing.

"Things are looking up," Katy thought.

Chapter 12

Robbie stood and watched, while Jeff spoke into the radio.

"Number three four seven zero, precedence P, papa, HXB twenty-four," he said, referring to a printed form lying on his desk. He was talking with the City of Bellevue Emergency Operations Center (EOC), passing along a formal message as a representative of this part of the neighborhood, requesting medical assistance for the injured people they'd just stabilized. The neighborhood medical team had helped these people move from life-threatening red status to yellow, still requiring urgent assistance but definitely better off.

Jeff was using the ARRL Radiogram [24] format, as he'd practiced in emergency exercises with the EOC previously. In some cases, the EOC would request assistance from the National Guard, via the state-level EOC in Camp Murray, just south of Tacoma. But for now, local help was probably all they'd get, at least until blockages in many major roadways were cleared.

Robbie stood, waiting patiently for Jeff to finish. Jeff didn't look up from his form. Even though he'd practiced before, it took all his concentration to ensure he read the message correctly.

All morning, Robbie rode his bike back and forth, taking direction from his father, and doing a good job of it. He knew it was important work, probably even lifesaving a couple of times, like when he'd delivered some critical supplies to the medical team when they ran low. But he felt like he could do more, make more of a difference. And compared to what he had done yesterday, taking care of his father and the rest of the family, this was a cakewalk. I'm ready for some real action, he thought.

Jeff paused for a moment and took off his headset.

"Whew! All this talking is wearing me out."

"All this waiting around is wearing me out," Robbie complained.

"You got to ride around earlier," Jeff said. "And whether you realize it or not, you're a huge help. Trust me, you're making a big difference. And you can't tell me you're bored, after all that's been going on."

"It feels like I'm not really helping much now," Robbie said. "There has to be something more important to do."

"The day is still young," Jeff said. "There will be plenty more fires to fight. I promise."

***

"Jeff, this is Katy, KE5HTI, checking in. Can you hear me?" Katy was standing on the dirt road in the greenbelt, holding her radio. It was the top of the hour, and according to the calling clock, time to check in again. She hadn't really expected anyone to answer, but it was still worth trying. She'd been walking uphill for the last hundred yards, and this location with its higher elevation might provide better reception than where she'd tried earlier.

There was no answer. She tried again. The plan called for checking repeatedly at the top of hour, in a ten-minute window.

"KE5HTI, this is Jeff, NM8J."

Katy jumped at the sound of Jeff's voice and almost dropped the radio.

"There's a little static," Jeff continued, "but I can make you out pretty well. Are you OK? Where are you?"

Katy was so happy to hear Jeff. The familiar voice was something safe, something normal. And since Jeff was healthy enough to operate the radio, this was great news all by itself.

"Hi Jeff! I'm so glad to hear your voice. I'm coming home from downtown, on foot. It's a total mess down here and probably not getting better soon. How are things in the cul-de-sac? Is that where you are? Is everyone OK? I'm so glad you're on the air!"

"Aside from a few cuts and bruises, everyone here is OK. We're trying to help people in the surrounding neighborhood as much as possible. There were some casualties, but nobody in our immediate area. We have a lot of blocked roads here, from trees, power lines, and crashed or abandoned cars. How is it there? Are you safe?"

"Like I said, downtown is a mess. There are a lot of people still waiting for help. Once they finally figure out it's not coming anytime soon, they're going to be even more upset, and they'll be heading into the suburbs for food and water."

"I'm surprised they haven't all left already."

"They probably live far away. Anyhow, I'm heading your way now."

"Which route are you taking?" Jeff asked.

"I've been heading east in the power line greenbelt, parallel to NE 8th Street. But I still have to get around the North Lake neighborhood. I'm guessing things are bad there."

"Definitely. Don't even think about going through there. It's bad enough there when folks are comfortable and have their TVs on. If it's not already a nightmare in there, it will be soon."

"Yeah. I'll loop around to the north. It'll probably take a little longer, but it should be a lot safer. And besides, the roads heading directly east are really bad. There's a huge crack crossing 8th that's too wide to jump. I even saw cars in it at one point."

61

"Yeah, a lot of roads are cracked, although not that bad. Is there anything we can do to help?"

"I don't suppose there's any way you could come get me?" Katy asked, hopefully.

"I wish I could, but it looks like all roads leading that way are blocked. And if you're not in any immediate danger, we have some pretty serious issues around here we're still dealing with."

"OK, I'll keep heading your way and should be fine. Let's stay in touch. I'm glad you're taking care of things there. How about I check in every hour on this frequency?"

"Sure. If I don't hear from you, I'll assume something is wrong and I'll monitor constantly. Check in when you can. If I hear nothing for more than ninety minutes, I'll send help, if possible. Make sure you give me your location every time you check in, so I'll have a good idea where to look, if you end up running into trouble. Hold on one sec."

Katy waited.

"I just checked 147.560 megahertz, and it's open for now. Let's use that as a dedicated frequency. I have another channel I can keep open on my radio here, so I'll just leave it assigned to you for now. Call in anytime you like."

"That sounds like a good plan," Katy replied. "For now I'm going to keep heading east and I'll check in with you in an hour. Give me a minute to make sure I can reach you on the new frequency. Hold on."

Katy added the new frequency to her radio's memory bank and then tested by transmitting.

"KE5HTI for NM8J."

"I hear you clearly," Jeff replied.

"OK, it's time to get going. Talk with you shortly."

"OK. Stay frosty. NM8J monitoring."

Frosty? Katy shook her head. It must be guy talk for "cool."

"KE5HTI, uh… frosty and… clear." Katy shut off her radio and stuffed it into her purse, so she could reach it easier, without having to take off her backpack.

She set out again, down the gravel road, this time with a spring in her step.

Chapter 13

Things weren't going Neil's way. The most obvious route, northward on I-405, wasn't a safe option anymore. More than once, Neil had been forced to slowly navigate through massive car pileups that completely blocked the road. But that wasn't the worst of it.

Half of a mile back, Neil had paused while approaching another pileup, then ducked out of sight to observe a group of five men on the other side of the wreckage, about fifty yards ahead. Two were climbing inside a Ford Taurus, and three more were breaking windows on other cars. They were looters.

Neil watched intently as the driver, who'd been patiently waiting for someone to come to rescue him, was now sprinting to the north, a terrified look on his face, as another man chased him away with a crowbar.

Neil adjusted his position and squatted beside a crumpled sedan. He peered around the bumper, watching the men closely. They were efficient, smashing windows, rummaging around, and moving on to the next car. Slowly, they were making their way toward Neil's position. They looked pretty good at what they were doing. While it didn't mean they would be good at attacking and robbing him, the odds were good that if he tried to pass them, there would be trouble, and his main goal was to get home quickly and safely. He would have to change course. A minor delay would be worth avoiding an unnecessary fight.

When the men were still about forty yards away, Neil silently slipped back the way he'd come.

He quickly walked back along the highway, begrudging every step that led him further from Renee. He would have loved to hop over a fence, but as luck would have it, this part of the highway had a tall wall on the east side and a steep slope on the west side. But his luck wasn't all bad. After only a few dozen yards, he spotted something he hadn't noticed when heading north earlier.

Along some highways in the region, the designers called for tall, concrete walls to buffer adjacent neighborhoods from the constant traffic noise. This one had a door built into the concrete, to allow maintenance personnel to access the roadway from the other side.

Neil hopped over the concrete dividing barrier, walked around two parked cars, and stopped in front of the door, which was recessed into the wall. He dropped to one knee, removed his pack, and took out a sheaf of papers. It was his "Get Home Plan."[25] Among the papers was a set of maps that showed different pre-drawn routes through the area. He traced his way along one of them, trying to estimate his current position. He had a general idea, but it was difficult to know exactly where he was. He took his phone out of his pocket and turned it on. Although it showed no cellular signal, it was a smartphone, which was essentially a miniature computer that could make phone calls, connect to wireless networks, and most importantly in this situation, receive GPS signals. His phone had GPS software that didn't need a cell signal or constant wireless data connection to work, unlike many other popular applications. His application stored map data on the phone itself. After waiting a minute to lock onto multiple GPS signals, Neil could see his exact position. He could see on the map that a city street wasn't far from the other side of the wall, and that street led to thoroughfare that would lead him north.

Neil turned his phone off to conserve what was left of his battery, then packed up his paper maps. He reached to the door in the wall and tried the handle. It was locked, as he'd expected. He pulled a small, black pouch from his pack. It contained a series of slim, metal tools, several inches long with different shapes on their ends: his lock-pick kit.[26]

Neil selected a pick with a small bump on the end, and an accompanying tension wrench, bent at ninety degrees about a quarter of the way down. He slipped the tension wrench it into the cylinder and applied a small amount of pressure, enough to turn gently the lock if it were already unlocked. Then he slipped the pick into the cylinder and moved it back and forth gently for a minute, feeling his way along as he progressed. His luck was good. This lock was well-maintained and easy to manipulate. With a soft click, Neil felt the cylinder turn smoothly. The door was unlocked.

Neil smiled for the first time that day. Stowing his picks, he shouldered his pack, turned the door handle and stepped through the opening.

Chapter 14

Katy panned the binoculars back and forth, taking in as much as she could. There were more people outside now, talking in groups, escaping the darkness of their apartments and warming up in the morning sun. She could see the end of the greenbelt ahead. She would either have to cut through the outskirts of the neighborhood to the southeast, or change course and go northeast, even farther away from home. She sighed and put the binoculars back in her bag. Wondering how much longer it would take her to get home, she backed away from the bush she'd used as cover, and moved into the more thickly wooded area.

She paused at the end of the dirt road, where the green belt stopped, then cautiously approached the last of the concealing bushes. She could see some of the dense housing area ahead. Katy squatted and waited for several minutes, looking east. The buildings appeared to be remarkably intact, with only a few broken windows visible, and only one collapsed carport. She spied half a dozen men and three women on the stoop of an apartment building straight ahead. She couldn't make out what they were saying, but their voices were raised and one man kept pointing to the south. Moments later, they all got up and walked down the steps and headed south until they disappeared from view.

Katy tried to remember where the boundaries of North Lake were. It had to be farther south, right? This might not be the nicest neighborhood, but it appeared to be a lot better than the one she'd passed through earlier. Katy scanned with her binoculars, trying to recall newspaper articles and TV blurbs that described where the worst of the crimes in the city took place. It was tough to tell exactly where she was, or where the worst neighborhood ended and the less dangerous area began. What she was seeing didn't look so bad.

"I must be clear of North Lake now," she said to herself.

She wasn't.

Chapter 15

"Where is everyone?" Jimmy asked.

"They probably took everythin'. Ain't nothin' left. They went home."

Their day had been a success so far. They'd scored the box of food from their previous victim. Their next victims were two girls, each carrying two toasters, one under each arm. Rodney and Jimmy didn't have a use for four toasters, but taking them was fun.

Then there was the older boy, unarmed and smart enough to not risk serious injury, who'd given up his carton of cigarettes. And the last victims were two smaller boys who had been struggling down the sidewalk, sharing the weight of a used Dewalt chop-saw. This wasn't turning out to be a very productive approach after all.

The last score had been almost an hour before, and smoking cigarettes was getting boring. Either word had gotten out that this was a more dangerous route than the main road, or, as Rodney suggested, most of the good stuff was already gone. All of the ants were either back in the nest or scavenging farther away for their scraps.

"Nobody else is coming. And even if someone else came, their stuff would probably suck. What are we supposed to do with a stack of toasters? Plus, I'm hungry," Jimmy said. "We ain't had nothing to eat since those Slim Jims this morning. Let's go."

"Yeah, me too. Mama should make us a sandwich, since we've been so busy. We've been good boys!" Rodney said with a grin.

They got up from the pavement, where they'd been crouched behind a car, and started walking back toward their apartment. Halfway down the block, they turned into an alley, the shortest route home.

As came out of the alley, rounding the corner back onto the sidewalk, Rodney stopped.

"Check that out. Nice. More stuff for us. And that stuff looks good!"

Chapter 16

"Great," Katy thought, scowling.

Thirty seconds ago she'd stepped out of the bushes onto the sidewalk, after carefully scanning the area. Everything had been clear, smooth sailing until she'd made it about fifteen yards into the North Lake neighborhood. Then she'd heard voices and glanced back to see two young men emerge from the alley half a block away. Unfortunately, they also saw her.

Katy focused forward and walked faster. She knew she needed to avoid looking like prey, because from what she saw in their eyes, these guys looked like predators. She was confident and strong and had every right to walk on this sidewalk, she told herself. Momentarily emboldened, she held her head high and walked with a purpose, trying to put more distance between them without looking like she was running away.

The two men were still on the opposite side of the street, which meant that Katy could see them with her peripheral vision. They were keeping pace with her and making no effort to hide the fact that they were eyeballing her.

She got a better view as she maneuvered around some overturned garbage cans blocking most of the sidewalk. They were moving faster now, closing in, almost directly opposite her. Now Katy could hear them talking in hushed, menacing tones, but couldn't make out what they were saying.

Katy stopped. She turned to the side and looked at them squarely, with no visible emotion, to show them she was unafraid, hoping they would back off. Both men stopped.

"What's this fine lookin' woman doin' in our neighborhood, Jimmy?" Rodney called from across the street.

"Lookin' for a good time is my guess. And I think she likes us," Jimmy said, leering at Katy.

"Then we should show her a good time."

Katy turned and kept walking, realizing that stopping had been a mistake.

She clenched her fists and fumed. This was ridiculous. It had only taken her a minute to get into trouble after coming out of the greenbelt. Now she had two men following her! She pretended once again to ignore them and kept walking. But she felt like running.

Katy casually reached into her pocket and pulled out her key ring. In addition to her small flashlight, it held six keys.

With her other hand, she reached into her back pocket and pulled out the device she'd retrieved from her car trunk earlier that morning. She flicked a small switch and glanced down briefly to see whether the red LED was lit. It was. That meant it was ready to use. She gripped it tightly in her left hand as her right hand clutched her keys.

She clenched her fist. Katy had taken boxing classes for several months when she was younger, and after an uneventful but nonetheless terrifying encounter with a homeless man in a Seattle parking garage, she'd enrolled in a series of women's self-defense courses. She didn't end up sticking with martial arts as a hobby, but she did learn some basic techniques, including how to hit.

Increasing her pace even more, Katy momentarily relaxed her grip enough to position the key ring in her palm so that the keys stuck out from between her fingers. She tightened her fist again, the keys protruding like short metal claws, a technique she learned in one of her courses. If nothing else, she would make any attacker very uncomfortable.[27]

For a fleeting moment, she wished she'd prepared better before stepping out of the greenbelt. She should have taken the multi-tool out of her pack, opened the knife blade, and carried that instead of having to resort to keys. And now her pursuers were too close. She had no time to fish around in her bag.

Katy continued her quick pace. It didn't help.

The men jogged across the street and took up a position to her left, uncomfortably close.

"Hey babe, whatcha doing 'round here? You here to give us first aid?" Jimmy asked, jerking a thumb at the bright red backpack.

Katy didn't care about his question, and knew an answer wouldn't matter. She stopped and faced them, trying to keep her hands from shaking.

She knew she couldn't outrun them. She was done trying to avoid them. And although she was frightened, Katy's fear started to transform into anger. How dare they prey on her? They deserved what they were about to get.

Chapter 17

"Leave me alone! If you touch me, I'll hurt you. It's not worth it." She spoke with resolve, firmly, looking each one in the eye.

Jimmy laughed and lunged forward, hands outstretched. Just as he was about to reach her, Katy unexpectedly stepped forward and jammed her left hand into his abdomen, pressing the stun-gun's trigger a split second before it reached him. A jagged arc of electricity jumped between the two metal extensions on its end, and then it disappeared into his midsection. Jimmy's eyes widened in shock as he convulsed and doubled over.

The stun-gun was most effective when used to shock large muscle groups. The abdomen, covered with a sheet of muscle, was an ideal target. Katy knew that a violently contracting abdomen, in addition to hurting, made doing anything else a lot more difficult, just as vomiting did.

As 800,000 volts of electricity coursed through Jimmy's body, Katy drove forward again, holding the button down, intent on delivering more than a quick jolt. She needed him out of commission for as long as possible, to give her time to disable his companion and get away.

Jimmy let out a strangled moan, unable to catch his breath, and collapsed to the ground, curling into a ball and clutching his belly.

"Rodney, help!" he gasped, barely audible. Then he retched.

Rodney watched in stunned amazement.

"Stay back, Rodney," Katy warned, hoping that using the man's name would bring him to his senses. "You'll get the same if you come any closer." But he didn't appear to be worried. Scowling, he took a step closer.

No stranger to stun guns and how they felt, since the police had needed to restrain him more than once in the past, Rodney deftly avoided Katy's jab as the sound of arcing electricity filled the air. Katy stepped forward with the jab, but Rodney only moved to the side, effectively closing the gap between them. Now he was very close to Katy, too close.

He lashed out hard, catching her off-balance and smashing his fist into her forearm, causing her to drop the stun-gun at her feet. He wrapped both arms around her, lifted her off her feet, and threw her violently to the ground.

Katy landed on her back, hard. Luckily, her backpack cushioned the fall and prevented her head from hitting the pavement. But with the force of the fall, the zipper gave way and the backpack burst open, spilling her supplies onto the sidewalk. The impact also knocked the wind out of her, and she lay on the ground, trying desperately to pull air into her lungs.

Rodney squatted down next to her head and looked at her with detachment, as if she were a freshly-caught fish gasping in the bottom of his boat. He tilted his head to the side and smiled.

"You're in big trouble now, pretty lady."

Katy, still barely able to breathe, gathered all her energy and tried to sit up.

"Stay down," Rodney said, as he placed his palm on her forehead and pushed down hard, cracking the back of her head on the sidewalk. Katy lay and gasped, tears streaming from her eyes from the pain. Rodney leaned over her, leering, his face inches from hers.

"You ready to stop causing trouble? Just stop fighting, come home with us, and we'll party."

75

Katy's right fist flew upward, with all the power she could muster at such an awkward angle. She felt the keys sink into his cheek and she pulled down hard.

Rodney fell back, his hands instinctively clutching his face as blood gushed from between his fingers. Katy rolled over and grabbed the stun-gun. She stood up groggily, trying to clear her head and catch her breath.

The fight was over. All she wanted to do was get away. She was done with the fight. Now it was time for flight. Katy turned to run.

Suddenly, Katy found herself face-down on the sidewalk. A hand clutched her pant leg.

Katy rolled onto her back and tried to scramble backward, dropping the stun gun in her attempt to get away from Jimmy, who had recovered enough to grab her. She wasn't fast enough. Jimmy grabbed her other leg and hauled himself on top of her, pinning her down.

His reddened, enraged face was inches from hers. She felt his hand reaching down to struggle with his waistband, then Katy saw the shiny blade of a knife moving upward, toward her face.

Instinctively, she brought her arms up to shield her face as her self-defense training kicked into gear. Without thinking about it, she twisted her hips slightly, to give herself a small area to move within, then rammed her knee upward as hard as she could, three times in rapid succession, into his groin, like a piston firing in an engine, driven by the explosive force of her fear and anger. Jimmy gasped and rolled off to the side, lying on the ground, just a few feet away from Rodney. Both of them lay there, whimpering. Jimmy gagged.

Katy picked up her stun gun. Rodney didn't appear to care. With one bloody hand extended toward Katy and the other clamped to his torn cheek, he rose to one knee, then stood and staggered toward Katy, cursing.

Katy punched the stun gun into the side of his neck and he dropped to the ground.

Katy ran.

After sprinting several blocks, zig-zagging down side streets, she paused to catch her breath. Her frantic pace was going to attract attention if it hadn't already. Reluctantly, she slowed to a walk, and a wave of dizziness swept over her.

She turned left, headed east. "This should be the right way," she thought as she panted, trying to suck in enough oxygen. "Just a few more minutes and I should be out of here."

An explosive wave of nausea hit. Katy bent over and vomited.

Running didn't usually make her feel like this. Maybe it was the adrenaline. Then Katy noticed wetness on her hand. Confused, she looked down and was shocked to see her right arm was covered with blood.

Chapter 18

Neil walked and walked. Two times in the past half hour he'd been approached by a handful of men who must have thought he was a good target. And both times he'd pulled up the hem of his shirt to reveal the holstered .45 handgun perched on his hip. Each time, the men had scattered, in search of an easier target.

Although he was unscathed, it was a bad plan. The neighborhood was getting increasingly worse, the farther north he walked. Earlier he'd been passing well-kept, modest homes, but now he was passing dirty, broken-down homes, complete with barking dogs in weed-ridden yards, blocked by chain-link fences.

As individual homes gave way to apartment buildings, he wondered whether he'd be better off returning to the highway. The faces he encountered scowled at him, but he ignored them and kept walking.

He knew didn't fit in. His purposeful stride, the intense look in his eye, and the resolve anyone could read from fifty yards away all said "Stay out of my way." While it kept trouble away, his approach still attracted attention, and that was the last thing he wanted.

Neil tried to stay away from the main roads, and from time to time he zigged east or zagged west by a block or two, doing his best to avoid any groups of people. But every step that wasn't due north irritated him.

He thought back to the plans he made to get home. He had neglected to factor in crime statistics by area, and while he had expected to have to avoid people from time to time, he hadn't expected to feel like a soldier in enemy territory.

Neil stopped next to a vacant lot, its waist-high weeds nearly covering several mounds of garbage and two rotting mattresses. He didn't see anyone in view, so he simply sat down in the weeds, using them for cover. He needed a minute to check his radio again. He didn't like stopping in this area, but he wanted to try calling Renee one more time.

Just as before, there was no reply. This time, after putting his radio back in his pack, he pulled out a different radio, a scanner, and pressed a sequence of buttons that set it to scan UHF and VHF amateur radio frequencies. He wanted to know if anyone local was on the air. Since the scanner had plenty of battery power left, so he could afford to let it scan as he kept moving north. If he was fortunate enough to find a local ham radio enthusiast, he could always retrieve his radio and get some advice on the best route out of the area. He clipped the scanner to his belt,[28] shouldered his pack, and started walking.

Chapter 19

Katy tried to slow her breathing. Rodney must have sliced her arm when they were struggling. It was bleeding profusely, and she could feel a throbbing pain that seemed to momentarily intensify with each heartbeat. Katy gingerly pulled up her sleeve and examined the wicked gash across the skin of her outer forearm, just below the elbow. She very slowly clenched her fist and released it. Her fingers still worked, but the pain intensified as the muscles moved under the wounded tissue. Without warning, Katy vomited again, expelling the remains of her meager breakfast onto the sidewalk. She retched a few more times, but nothing else came up.

Sudden vomiting was a bad sign, she knew, and wondered whether she was going into shock. She coughed and spat.

Katy's dizziness increased and her knees weakened as she staggered forward. There was no way she could safely wait here, and she also couldn't expect anyone to call 911. She had to keep moving, to get somewhere safe, before the situation got worse.

Katy moved with a singular purpose now, focused entirely on survival. She urgently needed to attend to her bleeding arm, but also knew she needed to put more distance between herself and her attackers. She took deep breaths and focused on walking, one step at a time, moving one block south and one block east. With her left hand, she applied pressure to the wound and managed to stanch most of the blood flow. While that was an improvement, she still felt terrible, like she needed to throw up again. She had to stop and rest.

Katy stopped to get her bearings, looked around quickly and then ducked into an alley. She backed up to a dirty, brick wall on the far side of a stinking dumpster, then slid down until she was sitting on the ground. The smell of spoiled milk made her sensitive stomach roil, but at least she was out of sight and could rest for a few minutes. She hoped she would have the strength to get back up.

She shrugged off her backpack, intent on tending to her arm with the first aid supplies she'd stuffed inside earlier. And she badly needed a drink of water. As she carefully swung the bag off her shoulders and over her wounded arm, she noticed it felt oddly light. Now it sagged open on her lap and she stared at it in dismay. Inside were two candy bars and a package of AA batteries. She thought back to the scuffle and swore under her breath.

Katy forced herself to be calm, to think. Suddenly, she remembered her small purse, which she had looped over one shoulder and across her body. Amazingly, the small strap had survived the ordeal. At last, some welcome news. She still had her wallet, her cell phone, spare change, odds and ends, but nothing she could use to treat her arm. But the purse also held her radio.

She pulled it out and the flexible whip antenna sprung free. Then turned it on and immediately pressed the transmit button.

"NM8J, this is KE5HTI, can you hear me?" Katy said in a hushed voice. Seconds passed.

"Katy, this is Jeff. How are you doing? Is everything OK?" he asked, concern in his voice. Katy exhaled in relief.

Katy collected her thoughts and spoke, trying to be as clear and concise as possible.[29]

"I was attacked by two guys. One of them had a knife and cut my arm, but I got away. I lost my first aid kit..." she paused for a moment before adding "and my water."

Mentioning it made it worse. She suddenly noticed how thirsty she was. The combination of stress, adrenaline, fighting, the blood loss, and the rush to escape left her mouth feeling as dry as a sandbox.

"Are you safe now?" Jeff asked, his voice urgent. "Are the guys anywhere nearby?"

"I don't think so. I hit them both with a stun gun."

"Good. They probably deserved worse. How bad is your cut?" he asked.

"I stopped the bleeding with pressure," Katy replied. "But I'm concerned it'll start bleeding again if I don't keep the pressure on, especially if I start moving again. And I feel a little sick to my stomach," she admitted.

"OK, you could be going into shock. You may want to lay down if you can, and prop your feet up on something. Can you wait there for someone to come get you?"

"I'm a few blocks from where I was attacked, and I don't think the men were in any condition to follow me. It looks like I'm out of the worst part of this neighborhood, and I'm closer to you than when we talked last. I remember seeing houses to the south, just before I turned into this alley."

"Will you be safe where you are?"

"I don't know. Probably. I'm out of sight of the road."

"We can't drive down to that area. The roads are blocked. I think we can send a first aid kit and water, though. Do you think you'd be able to walk out after resting?"

"If I can take care of my cut, rest for a few minutes, rehydrate and get my energy back, I think so. Um... but I'm not exactly sure where I am now. I was running, and then I turned..."

"Hold on a minute. We'll figure it out. I'll be back in a minute, OK?"

"OK. I'll stay out of sight and sit tight."
"Back in a minute. NM8J."
"KE5HTI monitoring."

Chapter 20

"I can do this Dad," Robbie said confidently. "You know I can. And you have plenty of help around here now. You don't need me like you did earlier."

There were at least two more people in the neighborhood who needed medical help, and the medical team was en route. And there was a house fire two blocks away. Everyone they could find to help was already fighting to keep it from spreading. Jeff still had a lot to coordinate. He couldn't leave his post without putting lives at risk. Marie was doing her best to help, but still had to keep an eye on Robbie's little sister, Lisa. At this point, it looked like Robbie was the only person available to run a first aid kit and water over to Katy, but Jeff and Marie didn't like the idea of Robbie going anywhere near a bad neighborhood in these conditions.

"Robbie, more than anything, we want to keep you safe," Marie said. "If it looks like there is any real danger between here and there, you aren't going. It's that simple. I know you want to help, but we have to talk it through and look at our options. We don't want you getting hurt."

"In other words, we aren't letting you into the mess to the west unless we know you'll be safe," Jeff added.

"You can trust me to take care of myself. You've seen that yesterday and today. You even said I'm grown up now, Dad," Robbie said defensively. "Plus, I've been doing this same thing already, all morning. Katy's just a little farther away." He paused for a moment. "I know I need to be careful. You can trust me."

Jeff sighed. The boy made a good point. He was growing up so fast, probably too fast lately. And this situation was unusual. Katy was in real danger.

"Hold on a sec." He swiveled back to face the radio.

"Katy, we're trying to work out a plan. Do you have any better idea where you are? Can you give me your location?"

"I'm not sure, but I think I can find out," Katy replied tersely. "Give me a minute."

"Monitoring."

Katy climbed to her feet slowly, fighting the dizziness that threatened to topple her. She stumbled out of the alley, searching for a street sign and a building number. At the intersection to the north, she could just make out the lettering on the small, green street sign. One down. Now for the building number. She turned around and looked at the two closest buildings. There was nothing visible on the building to the left. But on the right, faded plastic numbers nailed to the red wall read "14309." She turned and walked back into the alley.

"Jeff, I'm right by 14309 Southeast 3rd Avenue. It's a two-story, dark red apartment building."

***

Jeff and Robbie looked at the map on the wall and pinpointed Katy's position.

"Robbie, what are the biggest dangers between here and North Lake?" Marie asked.

"Well, If I'm on my bike, I have to watch out for any downed power lines," Robbie said, thinking quickly. "And fallen trees. And I should stay away from any fires, which shouldn't be a problem on the main roads. They're wide and my bike is skinny.

I should be able to go just about anywhere." He paused, and Marie and Jeff looked at him expectantly.

"People are probably my biggest concern," he continued. "If they're hurt or mad about something, they may want to take it out on me. But I'll be moving pretty fast and I should be able to avoid them. Besides, people between here and there are probably not going to be that bad, not like down here," he said, pointing to the center of North Lake.

"And I can take a gun," he said, matter-of-factly.

"No way!" Jeff and Marie blurted simultaneously.

"I know you're fourteen, and you're ahead of your years," Jeff said. "But if I thought it was so dangerous you'd need a gun, there's no way I'd let you go in the first place." Jeff hesitated, and looked at the map again. "I think you're right. The people between here and North Lake shouldn't be a threat. That said, you should definitely carry a can of pepper spray. And you'll have a knife, but that's for practical reasons. You shouldn't need that for self-defense."

Marie nodded in agreement as Jeff spoke, then added, "If it even looks dangerous, you come back. It's that simple. Will you promise me?"

"OK, I promise. If it looks really dangerous, I'll come back. But don't worry, I'll be safe." He grinned. This would be so much more interesting than running errands in the neighborhood.

"All right, then. Hurry up and pack your bag, and I'll check it before you go," Jeff said. He turned back to his radio and transmitted.

"Katy, I have an update."

Robbie ran upstairs to his bedroom. He grabbed the backpack he'd thrown on the floor the night before. It still contained the gear from their ill-fated camping trip. He needed to pack for a different kind of trip now. He dumped it out on the floor. His mountain trail map wouldn't be of any use, and he definitely wouldn't need his camp stove, mess kit, and his multiple fire starters.

One by one, he packed the items he thought he'd need, filling the bag about halfway.

Robbie was ready for inspection. He sat at the kitchen table while Jeff went through his pack.

"OK, what are the most important things you packed? What do you need to prepare for?"

Robbie was ready. He was used to his dad quizzing him about this kind of stuff.

"People, weather, getting thirsty, and communication."

"Sounds good," Jeff said, grinning, proud of how levelheaded Robbie was being, even in the excitement. He pulled out Robbie's rain jacket, two bottles of water, a can of pepper spray, Robbie's handheld ham radio and backup battery, extra AA batteries, a water purifier, a pocket-sized first-aid kit, and a mini survival kit.

He checked the date on the pepper spray.[30]

"Good," he pronounced. "It doesn't expire for another year. What about these batteries? Are they from a fresh pack?"

"Yep," Robbie confirmed. "I got them from the drawer in the kitchen earlier."

"OK. What else do you have?"

"I have my Spyderco,[31] an LED flashlight, and a small compass in my pockets. In my bike panniers I have a big first aid kit, plus extra gauze, saline, and other first aid supplies, from earlier today. By the way, I have a rough idea of where I'm going, but I don't know if we have a road map of the area. Do you have one I can use?"

"Yeah, just a sec," Jeff said. He headed back to his office.

"I know you just ate lunch," Marie said, "but Katy might be hungry, so take an MRE." She set one down on the table in front of him.

"Good idea," Jeff said. "Plus they have toilet paper in the little accessory packet. You never know. That's way better than wiping with a leaf, or an old piece of newspaper."

"Knock it off," Marie chided.

"You mean, I might need to poop?" Robbie asked, grinning. Jeff grinned back.

Marie rolled her eyes. Typical boys and their poop talk. "Quit messing around, boys," Marie said, looking straight at Jeff as she emphasized the word "boys." "Robbie has a mission. Get serious and get moving."

Robbie stuffed the MRE and everything else except the radio back into his backpack.

"I'm ready to go."

"You still have your flat tire kit and pump on the bike, right?" Jeff asked.

"Yeah. And the water bottle is full too. Can I go now?"

"Check in every thirty minutes," Marie said. "No exceptions. If you don't check in, we're going to think something is wrong."

Robbie recognized her tone. This was the wrong time to argue.

"Check this out, Mom." He pushed some buttons on his Casio G-Shock digital watch, then held up his arm so she could see the display, which read 29:57. "Twenty-nine minutes and fifty-seven seconds, counting down. Every thirty minutes the timer will go off. Good enough?"

"Yes," Marie grinned, mussing his hair affectionately. "That's my boy."

"When it goes off, it might take a couple of minutes for me to stop whatever I'm doing and get to my radio, so don't freak out if I'm a little bit late, OK?"

"I will freak out, so do me a favor and be on time."

"OK, Mom. Let's do a radio check." He turned on his Yaesu VX-8R, waited a moment, and pressed the transmit button. "Testing, KE7CTA."

The handheld radio sitting on the table broadcast his voice clearly, and started to produce a feedback whine.

"The radio is good," Jeff said. "You should have no problem with the range. We've tested these all the way to downtown Bellevue and they were clear. But remember, in some dips in the terrain, you could lose the signal. So if we can't hear each other, try getting to higher ground. You won't be going that far, so you should be fine. Also, this is the same frequency that Katy is using, and she'll be happy to hear from you too. Don't be surprised if you hear her calling while you're on the way. Now let's look at the map."

"Hold on, Dad," Robbie said. "A radio test is a two-way street, right? I need to make sure it can receive too."

"Oops. Sorry, I totally spaced," Jeff said. He picked up his handheld and transmitted. Robbie's radio worked as expected. "Good. All set. Now back to the map." He spread it on the table.

Jeff, Marie, and Robbie looked closely at the Bellevue street map.[32]

"This is probably your best route," Jeff said, as he marked a side road leading out of their neighborhood with a pencil, and drew a line straight down NE 8th Street. "And we all know about the North Lake neighborhood. Do not go through it. Don't even go near it." Jeff circled it on the map. "You have a couple of options," he added, and drew two more lines, forking the route as it moved westward. "You can decide which looks best when you get there. I got the address from Katy. She's right here." He marked the street and wrote the building number. It was just east of the North Lake area.

Robbie folded the map and put it in his backpack.

"I think you're better off with that in your pocket, Robbie. If you lose your pack for some reason, or lose your radio and other gear, your map will be a lifeline, especially in unfamiliar territory."

"Makes sense." Robbie retrieved the map, then stuck it into his inner jacket pocket.

"Promise me you'll stay safe," Jeff said, his voice cracking slightly. "That's your top priority. Katy needs you, and you're smart and fit and can take care of yourself, but your safety is more important. Promise me you'll use your head."

Robbie could tell his father was serious.

"I promise."

Minutes later, they all stood outside near Robbie and his bike. Marie stood behind Jeff, watching. A tear appeared in her eye and she quickly wiped it away.

"Don't worry, Mom. I'll be fine. I'll take a quick ride, help Katy get patched up, and escort her back. We'll both be safe and sound in an hour or two."

"Yes, you'll be fine. Go do good things, Robbie."

"Love you, Mom."

Robbie put on his helmet, shouldered his backpack, and gave a quick wave as he pedaled away on his mountain bike. He glanced back over his shoulder. Jeff stood with his arm over Marie's shoulder, holding her close. They waved. Robbie turned his head forward. They watched as he turned the corner and disappeared.

Chapter 21

Rodney gritted his teeth in frustration. His brother Jimmy lay on his bed, eyes closed groaning. Earlier, his mother had given him a bag of partially frozen corn, to use as an icepack on his groin. That was it. Calling 911 didn't work, so all they could do was wait.

Rodney stared at his reflection in the bathroom mirror. His mother had applied a bandage to his punctured cheek and it covered most of the side of his face. A blotch of red stood out in the center. He felt his anger burning, a white-hot ball in his gut. He was going to find the girl who did this to him and teach her a lesson.

"I'm out, Mama," he yelled, slamming the door behind him.

Fifteen minutes later, he sat in a car with two of his friends.

Of them handed him a small, heavy object, wrapped in an oily rag.

"Here you go," the man said. "Why do you need this now?"

"It's dangerous out there," Rodney said, handing him a roll of cash. "And we might have a lot more valuable stuff soon." He removed the black revolver and looked at it closely. "Does it work?"

"Of course it works, stupid," the man said. "I don't sell guns that don't work."

Andrew Baze

A truck pulled up next to them, as Robbie stuck the revolver in his waistband. Two men got out and walked up to the window.

"What's up?" one of them asked. "I hear you have a big score for us."

"I saw her last week, when I was watching the jewelry store on 8th. I think she's a courier or something. She always carried a briefcase and looked nervous. I saw her earlier today when I was looking for stuff downtown. She was leaving the store with the red backpack. I think she has all of the jewelry from the store, so nobody can steal it. And I know she's not far from here. I saw her a few minutes ago, but I was on foot and lost her."

"Nice," one of the men said. "That's got to be worth a lot more than the junk I took this morning. Count me in. What's the split?"

"Fifty-fifty, whatever's in the pack, with whoever finds her and holds her for me," Rodney answered. "And get the word out. Tell everyone you know, if they help you spot her, I have tons of good stuff. I can get cigarettes, a new TV, and whatever else they want."

"Hey, what happened to your face?" another one of the men asked.

"A piece of glass cut me when I smashed a window earlier," Rodney said with a scowl. "I'm fine. Shut up about it."

"Whatever," the man replied. "Just make good on our deal." He turned and walked back to the truck.

The truck's tires chirped as it pulled out. The car followed moments later.

Chapter 22

Katy felt a little bit better after her short rest, and thought about continuing her trek home. Even though she was pretty well concealed behind the dumpster, anyone walking up the alley would see her, and she didn't feel like dealing with anyone else. She felt vulnerable just sitting there, and decided to improve her situation.

She crept to the alley entrance and looked around. The coast was clear. She stepped onto the sidewalk and headed south. A minute later, she reached the end of the block and crossed the street. She would update Jeff in a minute, she thought, when she had a better idea of which route she was going to take.

As Katy slowly crossed the street, she scanned right and left. Two blocks to her right, she saw four young men striding into the intersection. To her horror, one of them pointed at her and shouted. The men all turned and stared at her.

The red backpack! Katy cursed. It made her too easy to spot. She should have left it in the alley, since it was practically empty anyway.

The men were too far away for Katy to tell, but she wondered whether one of them might be one of the men she had fought with earlier. Maybe they were part of a gang. It didn't matter. This new group of punks was clearly looking for her, and thanks to the bright red beacon of a backpack, they'd found her.

The four young men broke into a run. Without thinking, Katy dashed across the street, just out of their line of sight, up to the closest doorway, the front of a four-story apartment building. She heard their shouts getting closer.

She pushed the entry door open and flinched when the smell hit her. The lobby was filthy. She ignored it and darted to a nearby door marked "Stairs," pushed it open with her left arm and ducked inside the stairwell. There was nowhere else to go but up. Weak and fighting waves of nausea, Katy grasped the railing and pulled herself upward, step by step.

The exertion had reopened the wound on her arm. As Katy stopped on the second floor landing to catch her breath, she glanced downward and saw drops of blood on the concrete floor, leading back down the stairs. They clearly marked her trail.

Katy wasn't sure her pursuers would be perceptive enough to notice the trail of blood, but decided to take advantage of the situation. Katy smeared her bloody hand on the metal door and the door handle, trying to make it impossible to miss. She only had seconds before someone might come looking in the stairwell. She entered the second floor hallway and left several handprints along the right wall, as if she'd needed to brace herself. Then she touched the two closest doors, leaving more handprints. After that, she threw her backpack down toward the far end.

Katy stumbled back into the stairwell. Careful to keep pressure on the wound and not leave another blood trail, she headed up the stairs again. Seconds later, she was on the third floor. She opened the door with her clean hand. As she stepped through, she heard the crash of a door being flung open below, followed by a voice echoing through the stairwell.

"She's gotta be up here," someone cried. Another voice shouted, "Look! Blood! She went this way! Come on!" Footsteps thudded up the stairs.

Katy pulled the third-floor door behind her, cushioning it as it shut, her heart racing. She prayed her ruse would work. Then turning to survey the hallway, she saw something that made her heart race even faster.

Chapter 23

Katy watched with wide eyes as a man ambled slowly down the hall, moving away from her. The windows at each end of the building provided enough light for her to see he was wearing a blue, one-piece utility outfit, and he was pushing a bucket with a mop. He hadn't bothered to turn around as she opened and shut the door, and was probably doing his best to ignore the residents with their nonstop questions about power, water, and whatever else they mistakenly thought he could do for them. She was surprised he was out here at all, instead of holed up in his own apartment, pretending to not be home.

She was lucky this time. Not only did the maintenance man not appear to notice her, the door he had just walked away from was still swinging shut with a long, slow squeak.

Katy darted forward quietly, and covered the distance between herself and the door in just over two seconds. Just before it closed, Katy stuck her hand into shrinking gap, pushed the door open, and slid into the room. The door shut completely behind her, taking the last of the dim light with it. She stood, breathing heavily in the darkness.

Katy couldn't see a thing. She fished around in her pocket and pulled out her key ring. She felt for the tiny flashlight[33] and turned it on. The tiny light shone brightly and illuminated the room.

Now Katy saw she was in a narrow, dingy supply closet. There were shelves along the side walls, full of cleaning supplies, paper towels, spare light bulbs and other supplies. And things were looking up. On the rear wall sat a deep, utility sink, with two mops and buckets off to the side. Water!

Before Katy looked around more, she checked the door. The pushbutton lock was engaged, so unless the maintenance man came back, she would be OK.

She set her flashlight down on a shelf, so it illuminated most of the room. She quickly surveyed the supplies in the room and found a small stack of towels. She took one that looked stained but relatively clean, and pressed it against her arm. She needed to make sure the bleeding stopped as soon as possible.

Katy released the pressure for a second as she grabbed another small towel. She rolled it into a small cylinder and placed it under her arm. She pressed her arm against her torso, so the rolled towel put pressure on the brachial artery that ran down her arm. Hopefully, this combined with the direct pressure of her hand holding the towel over the wound would be enough to stop the bleeding.

Exhausted, Katy sat on the cold, dirty concrete floor and closed her eyes, fighting off another wave of dizziness. She didn't know whether it was normal to feel this way after a massive amount of adrenaline was dumped into her system, or whether it was a result of blood loss. There was nothing she could do about either one, and she sat with eyes closed, trying to keep from feeling sick.

A minute later Katy heard a crashing sound, immediately followed by a scream. It came from below her and to her left, back toward the stairwell she'd just used. It was very loud, and the thin floors and walls made it even easier to hear everything that went on in the building. Her bloody handprint ruse had worked, but she felt bad for the people in the apartments whose doors she'd marked. Another crashing sound sounded, this time followed by yelling and the sound of breaking glass. Only one more door left.

Seconds later, she heard a third crash, and silence. Maybe that apartment was empty.

Would they give up?

Chapter 24

The third floor stairwell door crashed open with a bang, followed by angry voices in the hallway. At first, Katy couldn't make out what they were saying, but the voices grew louder as the speakers approached the closet.

"She's gotta be here. Keep looking."

She froze, recognizing the voice. It was Rodney. She was sure of it. He must be standing right in front of her door, talking to someone farther down the hall.

"I'll check this floor. You check the stairwell on the other side, and you two take the top floor. We don't want her getting out the back."

Suddenly, Katy realized that light from her flashlight might be visible under the door. As fast as she could, she grabbed the flashlight to turn it off, and cringed as the keys on the ring jingled slightly. She cursed under her breath as she turned the light off, then stood in the darkness, holding her breath, afraid to move.

A voice spoke on the other side of the door.

"She could be in here." Katy heard the doorknob rattle. She didn't move. The door shook violently.

"You moron," she heard Rodney say, "Can't you see it's locked? How would she have a key? She must have gone back downstairs on the other side."

Katy heard the men continued to argue as they moved farther down the hall.

She took shallow, quiet breaths, still terrified of making a sound. Moments later, she heard the welcome sound of a door slamming shut at the far end of the hallway. She counted to sixty, making sure nobody returned, then turned the flashlight back on. She quickly grabbed several rags from the closest shelf and stuffed them around the base of the door, to prevent any light from escaping. Cautiously, Katy pulled her radio from her purse. Her hands were shaking. She turned the volume to its lowest setting, then turned it on. If she put the speaker up to her ear, she could hear clearly, but nobody more than two feet away would be able to hear anything, especially on the other side of the heavy door.

She transmitted in a loud whisper, hoping it would be comprehensible.

"This is Katy. Can anyone hear me?"

She waited ten seconds and tried again. There was still no answer. What was going on? Where was Jeff? He promised he'd monitor this frequency. She double-checked, making sure she was using the right one. Yes, it was still set on the same frequency. She thought for a moment. The logical explanation was that the walls of this building, including the floor above her, prevented her radio's signal from reaching Jeff's antenna. If this was the case, she was in trouble.

How would Robbie find her? What if he crossed paths with her attackers? How would she ever get out of here?

Chapter 25

Robbie picked up speed as he crested the hill and began descending. The road was surprisingly clear. There were no parked cars or fallen power poles, just open road. It looked completely normal, almost untouched. Aside from some people clearing debris from around a collapsed carport, it looked as if the quake hadn't even hit here.

He crested another small hill and the view changed. He braked as he approached the scene of an accident. He came to a stop alongside the first of three empty, demolished cars, and looked inside. The front seats and the dashboard were coated with a fine, white powder. Robbie was puzzled for a moment. He looked at the steering wheel. There was an odd-looking hollow section in the center, and a white sack sagged beneath it. Robbie recalled something his father had told him about what happened when an airbag went off. Aside from a panel shooting out from the force of a small explosive charge behind it, white powder blew everywhere as the bag deployed. The powder kept the airbag from sticking to itself while it spent years compressed inside a steering wheel. His dad had pointed out that while it was somewhat dangerous to get hit by the flexible panel that covered the airbag, and even the bag itself, neither of those things was as bad as hitting one's face on the dashboard or steering wheel.

Robbie looked away, feeling guilty. He wasn't on a sightseeing tour. There would be many interesting and unusual things to stop and look at, but he was on a mission. His father would have told him to stop dawdling and keep moving. He started pedaling down the hill again, focused on getting to Katy.

He couldn't help but wonder whether the drivers were injured, and where they went. If airbags went off in the cars, they probably weren't dead, but they could still be hurt. There were plenty of undamaged houses in the area. Maybe the drivers were taking shelter in one of them. He hoped the people were helping each other around here, as they were in his neighborhood.

Robbie reached the bottom of the hill and began making his way up the next one. It was more tiring than he'd expected. His thighs started to burn and his pace slowed, but he kept pushing.

At the top of the next hill he glanced at his watch and decided to take a quick break. He got off the bike, took off his pack and stretched his legs. He looked around but didn't see much activity, aside from a handful of people halfway up the next hill, who were struggling to clear wreckage from one of collapsed houses. It felt weird to watch and not help, but he knew that helping Katy was his top priority.

"*Beep, beep, beep,*" his watch chimed. It was time to check in.

Robbie pulled the radio out of his pack and keyed the transmit button.

"KE7CTA calling NM8J."

"KE7KFT here. What's happening? How are you doing?" his mother asked.

"I'm fine, on the hill at NE 8th and 145th. Nothing more than a few collapsed houses and a car wreck, and nothing in my way."

"OK. Looks like you have a couple more miles before you get to Katy. By the way, your dad hasn't been able to raise Katy on the radio, and we're not sure what's going on with her. Hopefully it's just a temporary reception problem. Remember," she cautioned him, "if it looks dangerous, come back. And don't waste any time."

Robbie felt guilty again for having stopped to look at the car wreck, and promised himself he wouldn't do that again.

"Got it, Mom, thanks. KE7CTA clear."

"KE7KFT monitoring."

Robbie turned off the radio and put it back in his pack, then hoisted it up and climbed back on his bike. He reached down and grabbed the water bottle from its carrier on the bike frame. After a couple of quick swallows, he wiped his mouth and put it back. It was time to move on.

Chapter 26

Robbie slammed on his brakes, frantically trying keep control of his bike as it started to skid. He pulled the front wheel to the side and slid to a stop sideways, only ten feet away from the thick, deadly snake blocking his path. He stared at it, terrified, afraid to move, flinching as he took a step to adjust his balance.

Robbie thought back to a class put on by the regional power company that had taken place the year before, at a search and rescue conference Jeff had attended. Robbie thought it would be fun to come along, so Jeff took him to a couple of classes. Two linemen showed the equipment they used to repair downed lines, talked about what caused transformers to fail, and described in detail what not to do when power lines were on the ground.

He remembered what happened when a live power line fed current into the ground. In many cases, a downed power line electrified, or as the instructors put it, "energized" the pavement or soil in the vicinity, even if it wasn't wet. That electrified pavement could extend several feet in all directions from the exposed cable. And that meant he could be millimeters from being electrocuted.

Robbie stood and panted, afraid to move. He looked around. He could see several houses nearby, none of which had any lights on or showed any other sign that their power was on. He took a deep breath, then started backing up, one step at a time.

The power line was still attached to the pole on the far side of the street and had fallen into the roadway when it snapped. The exposed end of the line lay about two-thirds of the way across the road, so Robbie walked his bike over to the other side and up onto the sidewalk. To give himself even more room, he pushed his bike through a flowerbed, lifted it over a foot-tall hedge, and pushed it across the front yard, a good distance away from the road. He turned toward the neighboring yard and kept walking parallel to the road.

Robbie heard a door open behind him.

"Hey, you! Kid! Get out of my yard!" he heard someone shout.

Robbie looked back quickly and saw a woman in a bathrobe, standing on her porch and waving a fist at him.

"Sorry!" he called, as he finished traversing the next yard and wheeled his bike back onto the sidewalk, leaving the downed cable a safe distance behind. Then under his breath, he said "Are you serious? You're worried about your lawn with all this going on?" Shaking his head in disbelief, he got back on his bike and began pedaling. He could still hear her yelling as he pedaled away.

Chapter 27

Robbie arrived at a bridge. More accurately, he arrived at what was left of a bridge. It reminded him of the cliff he'd encountered with his dad the day before, and he had no desire to approach it, much less look over the edge. It was time to detour. Robbie turned around and headed for the last side road he'd crossed, a block back. He turned into the small neighborhood, past the faded wooden sign that read "Hathaway Glen."

This neighborhood was similar to the others in the area. Due to its proximity to public housing, many people had moved away in the last several years, and property values had dropped. The result was predictable: more crime took place in this area, more garbage littered the sidewalks, and more houses sat vacant. It wasn't nearly as bad as public housing, but it was getting worse.

Robbie wasn't worried, though. His friend Josh had lived here not too long ago, and Robbie had ridden his bike over to visit several times, before they'd moved away. Robbie knew this area well enough, and knew what streets to avoid.

What Robbie didn't expect was to see so many people on the streets.

Most of the houses were constructed in the mid-1940s, and for whatever reason, most of the windows installed at the time were small. Even in the midday sun, little light made its way into the homes, so people went out to their front porches and yards.

Fortunately for these residents, almost all of the houses were intact. These people were lucky.

Robbie saw one group of people clustered around an old man holding a transistor radio. Apparently none of them had their own battery-powered radio to use, so this was probably their sole source of news.

Robbie rode past, waving to the people who looked toward him. They ignored him and looked back to the radio, as if they could get better news by using their eyes.

Robbie reached the end of the block and turned west. Two girls and a boy sat on the front porch of the corner house. One of the girls, the oldest of the children, had her arms around the younger ones, who were sobbing. Robbie's first instinct was to stop, but he reminded himself that finding Katy was his top priority. He couldn't afford to stop and help everyone along the way.

He hit the brakes. He had to do something. If nothing else, he would at least ask what was going on.

The older girl looked up, silent, as Robbie approached.

"What's wrong?" Robbie asked.

"My mom and dad are mad at us because we drank the last of the water."

"You don't have water? Isn't there anything else to drink?"

"There's only beer," she said, "and Daddy said we can't have any of it. We're thirsty. But when I tried to get some water from the faucet, only a little came out and then it stopped. Mommy and Daddy yelled at us and made us go outside." The girl's upper lip trembled.

Robbie frowned sympathetically. The power was out, the water was turned off, and people everywhere were starting to get thirsty. It wouldn't be long before many would start feeling hungry too.

Robbie took off his backpack. He hadn't brought much extra, but at least he had a home to return to, and his family was well-prepared for a situation like this. These kids apparently had nothing, and had no idea when water would be available again.

He pulled out a water bottle.

"Catch," he said as he threw it to the girl. She caught it and beamed at him.

"Sorry I don't have anything else I can give you," he added. "You should go listen to the radio with those people down the block there." He pointed back the way he'd come. "Maybe there's a shelter around here. You're going to need food and water, and it sounds like you don't have it at home. Good luck."

"What else do you have?" asked a voice behind him.

Robbie's head whipped around and he looked in dismay at the group of boys who'd appeared behind him.

"What do you mean?" Robbie asked. He glanced back at the three kids he'd just given the water to, but they were gone. That wasn't a good sign.

"You gave them water. We saw you. Lots of us don't have water now," another boy replied, whining. "We need some too."

"Time to share," another boy said, stepping forward. He was one of the older ones, and he was big. He was grinning but Robbie knew there was nothing funny about this situation.

"OK, sure," Robbie said with a big smile. The boy gave him a puzzled look. He hadn't expected this kind of reaction.

Robbie jumped onto his bike, taking advantage of the boy's momentary confusion, and started pedaling away from the group with all his might.

The older boys set off after him, like cats chasing a mouse. Robbie gained momentum, pedaling furiously. He chanced a quick look behind as one of the boys caught up with him. It was the big one, still grinning, and he'd just drawn up alongside Robbie. The grin turned to a scowl as he dipped his shoulder, ready to plow into Robbie and knock him off his bike.

Robbie recognized what was coming. He braked hard for a second, just before the boy threw himself sideways. It was perfectly timed. The boy, whose momentum was still carrying him forward, threw himself into mid-air, where Robbie should have been, tripped over his own feet, and landed hard on the pavement. The fall knocked the wind out of him and he lay there, gasping for breath, as Robbie started pedaling again. He sped away and didn't look back, ignoring the rapidly receding shouts and curses.

Heart pounding, Robbie leaned into the next corner at full speed. He zigzagged from block to block until he felt safe enough to slow down and catch his breath. At this rate he'd never have enough energy to last the day, and he still had a long way to go.

Chapter 28

Robbie hid his bike behind a patch of bushes. He ran the cable through the front wheel, through the frame, back through the rear wheel, then snapped on the padlock. It wasn't going anywhere. Bike secured, he walked over to the base of the water tower.

Robbie had tried to check in with his father. He was getting close to Katy's location, and wanted to get the latest information before riding in. Neither his father nor Katy had answered his calls. He remembered what his dad had said about getting to high ground, but he had no intention of going back up the hill he'd just come down, and he didn't want to go farther west, toward the really rough neighborhood. He looked up at the reservoir towering over him. This looked like the best and closest option.

"If I fall off a water tower, Mom and Dad are going to kill me, if the landing doesn't," Robbie muttered to himself as he looked up, planning his route. The ladder ascended from behind a locked cage. Robbie smiled. The cage was no obstacle to a motivated, experienced climber.

Robbie shook the cage. It felt stable. He tightened his backpack straps, scrambled nimbly over the cage and grabbed the ladder. He gave it a shake. It felt stable too. Robbie climbed up slowly. Fifty feet later, measured by the markings on the outside of the tower, he scrambled over the top of the tank.

There was no guardrail, other than a small, three-inch-high band of metal along the outer edge. The surface sloped downward slightly, so Robbie crawled forward on hands and knees, not comfortable enough to stand up. Yesterday's experience with his father falling over the cliff was a fresh reminder to play it safe.

Robbie reached the middle of the tank, where it levelled off enough to sit comfortably. He took off his pack and set it on the rusty surface.

"*Beep, beep, beep.*" His watch timer went off again.

"Well-timed!" he said aloud, as he opened his pack. He removed his radio and binoculars, then turned the radio on and transmitted.

"KE7CTA, checking in."

He waited several seconds, then heard the comfortingly familiar sound of his father's voice.

"KE7CTA, this is NM8J. I hear you clearly. Great signal. Are you on your way back already?"

"No, I had to climb up."

"Up where?"

"Um... up a water tower. Don't worry, it's safe. I'm right off NE 8th Street, not far from 150th. I couldn't reach you from down below, and I didn't want to backtrack up the hill. Plus, it gives me a good view of the neighborhood before I ride into it."

"That doesn't sound like a great idea, but what's done is done. Don't climb any more towers, be very careful on your way down, and don't tell your mother. Hold on while I check the map. I should be able to point you in the right direction."

"Wait! Have you heard from Katy? She's supposed to be on this frequency, right? I tried calling her too, and didn't hear anything. Have you heard from her?"

"No," Jeff admitted. "I tried too. No answer. Maybe she went indoors. The signal wasn't very strong the last time we talked, and if she went inside, that would probably be enough to block her signal. You will probably need to get closer to her to hear her. Hold on a sec."

Robbie carefully crawled closer to the edge of the tower, radio and binoculars in hand. He set the radio down carefully and put the binoculars to his eyes, looking down toward the dense housing area.

"We have your location," Jeff said. "This map shows the water tower. Look to the southeast at about 150 degrees. That's Katy's last known location."

"Hold on while I take another look," Robbie replied. He pulled the compass out of his shirt, where it hung attached to its 550-cord lanyard. He centered the red pointer on north and turned his body slightly, until he was aligned with the 150-degree mark, and looked through the binoculars again. He lowered the binoculars slightly and slowly lifted them toward the horizon, scanning as he went, trying to cover all the locations along this azimuth.[34]

He looked for alleyways that intersected with the main street. He saw a few likely candidates, but couldn't tell which one Katy might be in. He picked up the radio.

"I see a few areas where she could be hiding. How do I know which alley she's in? There are at least three dark red buildings. I don't want to waste time down there trying to figure this out."

"Hold on, Robbie. Let me see if I can find you a good landmark to narrow down the location."

Robbie scanned as he waited, and zeroed in on a building that looked like it might be the one Katy was near. Movement grabbed his attention. Six men walked down the sidewalk. Their heads were swiveling back and forth, like they were looking for something, or someone. The passed a two-story, dark red building.

"Dad? I think I might have found 14309. It's near a big intersection, main roads in all four directions. I see some people walking around." He didn't mention that the people looked like they were looking for someone. It might worry his father, and the last thing he wanted was for his father to order him to turn around and come home, especially when he was this close.

"It's on 135th Avenue Southeast," Jeff said, "at the intersection with Main Street. Can you see if the building is close to the next intersection to the east?"

"Yeah."

"That must be it, or very close to it. From what I see on the map, it looks like there are a few good routes between your location and Katy's, so choose whichever one looks safest. Get as much information as you can now, since you have a bird's-eye view. But don't wait too long. She needs your help."

"Got it Dad. Anything else before I sign off?"

"No. Just be smart. I have confidence in you."

"Thanks Dad. I'll talk to you again in thirty. KE7CTA clear." Robbie shut off his radio and restarted his countdown timer.

He pulled the map from his jacket pocket and spread it out on the metal surface of the water tower. He compared the map view with his real view and located the intersection of 135th and Main. He analyzed the main roads between his location and his destination, trying to figure out which would be easiest and safest to use. He would travel south on 140th, he decided. If he ran into trouble, he would reroute to the south and cut back up on a side street. He folded the map and stuffed it back into his pocket.

He took one more look at his target, trying to spot where the group of men had gone. He didn't see them, but he did see what appeared to be a garden shed engulfed in flames one block over. Nobody was trying to put it out.

After Robbie repacked his gear, he crawled back to the edge and started back down the ladder. He reached the cage at the bottom and carefully crawled over it. With about six feet between him and the ground, he lowered himself from the bottom side of the cage and dropped to the ground. He landed hard and lost his footing, sitting down hard. Fortunately, the soft earth cushioned his fall, so it wasn't painful.

But before he was able to stand up, the sound of voices greeted him from around the side of the tower, just out of sight.

"I heard something! I bet it's him," a boy's voice said. "Come on, let's get him!"

Chapter 29

Katy sat in the janitor's closet, eyes closed and trying to relax. Her right arm throbbed and her left hand was tired of applying pressure to the wound. She was afraid to let up. The last thing she needed was for the bleeding to start up again. She didn't know how much more blood she could lose before losing consciousness, and didn't even want to think about what might happen if the thugs found her unconscious.

The nausea had subsided, but now she had a headache, which she hoped was only due to dehydration, not from taking hard knocks to the head. She realized how thirsty she was. Her water bottles lay on the sidewalk somewhere. She looked at the utility sink and slowly got to her feet. She turned on the faucet and to her dismay, brown water gurgled out. Small particles collected in the water that pooled before it slowly drained. There was no way this water was potable. Looking at the sink itself, with brown and black stains coating the once white porcelain, it probably hadn't been drinkable even before the earthquake. Who knew what kind of contaminants were in it now? As desperately thirsty as she was, sat back down to wait, the radio on the floor next to her.

The doorknob rattled and Katy froze. It rattled again, but the lock held. Katy heard a muffled curse, followed by footsteps. There had to be many better targets than a janitor closet, but apparently someone had already decided that it was time to stock up on free cleaning supplies, paper towels or even a filthy mop. It was crazy what people would steal when they became irrational, Katy thought.

From time to time, she heard shouts and arguing. They were probably still fighting over unusable electronics. They would fight a lot more aggressively when they ran out of food and water, Katy thought, with grocery stores empty or guarded by police or heavily armed owners. With the power out, cash was the only usable currency, and most of these people probably didn't have much.

Katy stared at the radio. Nobody knew where she was. She hadn't updated Jeff after coming inside. She couldn't reach Robbie. He could be in that alley right now looking for her, and there was no way he'd find her. He might even be in danger. He was just a kid, she reminded herself. It wouldn't be easy to look for her without drawing attention to himself. She had to find a way to contact him.

She didn't know whether Jeff and Robbie were using the same frequency that she and Jeff had used. If he and Robbie were using a different frequency, the odds were slim that she'd find it. She thought about scanning the frequency band. That would allow her to hear anyone within range, but what if Jeff called while she was scanning other frequencies? Her radio could only listen to one frequency at a time,[35] and she couldn't risk missing Jeff's call. But if Jeff didn't call, what would she do?

Katy tried again. "NM8J, this is KE5HTI. Can you hear me?" She waited. There was still no answer. She checked her watch. It was just past three o'clock, and Jeff should be trying to reach her now. This was bad, really bad. She could feel the panic welling up inside.

She counted backward from twenty to zero, trying to relax further with each number. It helped a little, but the panic was still there. Katy transmitted again.

"NM8J, this is KE5HTI, do you hear me?"

There was no reply. Katy closed her eyes.

She would have to figure out something else to do. She tilted her head back against the wall, and tried to think. Leaving the same way she came into the building was not an option. She remembered the rear exit that the voice in the hallway had mentioned. She'd try that first. But when she got out, which way should she go? Her original path east through the neighborhood had been worse than she'd anticipated, and now she had an injury to complicate things. She couldn't move very fast. Running was out of the question. But she was not going to give up. There had to be a solution. There was always another option.

Katy turned off her flashlight to conserve the battery. Tired, thirsty, and weak, she sat in the dark and racked her brain.

Chapter 30

Neil had been travelling north on side roads, parallel to I-405, in order to avoid the empty cars and looters, until he reached I-90, the region's east-to-west artery. It blocked his path like a river. But instead of rushing water, the highway was full of cars and looters. In addition, access to the highway was limited by walls or tall fences topped with barbed wire.

Neil found a patch of fence behind a strip mall that had fallen into disrepair. The torn fence was out of sight of both the highway and the nearby surface streets, so it hadn't attracted anyone's attention yet. He waited until there were no scavengers in the immediate vicinity, scrambled down the bank, and jogged across the highway. Getting up the other side was easier. The only obstacle was a steep slope and a short, concrete wall, which had collapsed in several areas, creating ramps of dirt and rubble. He scrambled up the most stable-looking slope, hoping it was relatively settled, climbed over the remains of the wall, and down the other side.

According to his map, he could travel directly north for at least another five miles. Back on a surface street, with nobody in sight, he stopped and tried calling Renee again. Nothing. He was still too far away. He set his radio back to scan and clipped it to his belt. As he strode north again, he heard his first radio traffic of the day, a burst of static.

Chapter 31

Robbie backed quietly away from the tower, toward the bushes where he'd left his bike.

Three older boys appeared.

"Found him!" one of them shouted. They walked closer and stopped in front of him.

"You're in our hood," the tallest one said, "and we saw your bike. Give it up and we'll let you go. Otherwise..."

Robbie eyed the axe handles they each carried. They appeared to be brand new, with clean stickers still visible. Probably stolen earlier today, Robbie thought, glad they hadn't found actual axes.

"I don't have a bike," Robbie said, holding out his empty hands for them to see, trying to buy more time to think.

"My little brother saw you. It's gotta be around here somewhere." He pointed toward the closest patch of bushes, and motioned to one of the other boys. "Go look over there."

The boy disappeared into the bushes. Robbie thought about running, but he couldn't afford to give up his bike. He needed the supplies in his panniers. If it was just about his safety, he would have run and left the bike behind, but he couldn't leave Katy alone. She was injured and probably still in danger. She was counting on him.

"It's here," the boy called. There were sounds of breaking branches and cursing. "He locked the wheels. I can't roll it."

The leader glared at Robbie. "Where is the key?" he demanded, raising the axe handle. "Last chance. Give us the key and maybe we won't break your arms."

"OK," Robbie said, reaching into his side pants pocket and walking toward the boys.

The boys wore smug smiles now, knowing they'd won.

Robbie pulled his hand out, but instead of a key, it gripped a can of pepper spray. He didn't hesitate. He pressed the button on top of the canister and the expanding cone of pepper gel splattered across the leader's forehead and face.

Robbie knew what pepper spray felt like. Months ago, Jeff had tacked a sheet of paper to a tree and instructed Robbie to spray it with his can of spray. A gust of wind had blown some of the droplets back onto them both, resulting in coughing, sneezing, and burning eyes. Jeff had been laughing with tears in his eyes, but Robbie hadn't thought it was funny. It was worse than when he'd rubbed his eye after helping his mother chop some hot peppers. But that was nothing compared to what this kid had to be feeling now.[36]

This wasn't a fogger, which released many small particles in an expanding, cone-shaped cloud. Instead, this canister contained pepper gel, which was a lot thicker and didn't spread out as much. While it spread into a narrow cone as it flew toward its target, it didn't fill the air the same way the fogger did.

His dad had given him a large, Mace brand canister, the Magnum-3. After the second-long burst Robbie had just let loose, he probably had another fifteen bursts left.

As the surprised leader started gasping, the other two turned and looked at him, eyes wide. Robbie sprayed them too. The last one had been standing there with his mouth open, which made it even worse. The three boys rolled on the ground, grasping, choking and crying.

Robbie headed toward the fourth boy who had just emerged from behind the bushes, awkwardly carrying Robbie's bike. The boy stopped in his tracks.

"Set it down," Robbie instructed.

"You're dead meat," the boy replied, trying to sound menacing. But his shaky voice gave him away. He couldn't help but notice his friends wailing in the dirt. He set the bike down gently, raised his hands, and backed away, his eyes locked on the canister in Robbie's hands.

"I won't hurt you. Go ahead, take off," he said.

Robbie had a good idea what this kid would do with the axe handle if he let him go. He sprayed the boy with a long blast. Then he picked up the axe handles the boys had dropped and flung them into the woods.

Ignoring the boys' cries, he walked back to his bike. Heart pounding and hands shaking, he unlocked the cable, got on his bike, and headed down the path toward the main road.

Chapter 32

Robbie studied the map. The route he'd chosen earlier didn't look so good now. There were a lot more people out on the street than he'd expected, and most of them hadn't been visible from the water tower. And up to this point, his luck with the natives hadn't been good. He needed to get in and out quickly. He turned the map upside down and looked again, hoping the different angle would give him another idea. It didn't.

Frustrated, he closed his eyes, trying to clear his head. Looking down again with fresh eyes, he spotted something he hadn't seen before. A thin line extended north to south, bisecting the area and crossing all the major roadways. Robbie's eyes widened as his mouth turned from a frown to a smile. Why hadn't he thought of this before? He was staring at a path that was almost guaranteed to be clear of cars and people. It was a railroad track, now probably the safest road in town.

Robbie remembered something his mother had said not long ago, about how the city wanted to use the railroad land for something else when the train service had been discontinued, but the railroad company had some kind of special land rights that were difficult to take away, so the railroad track had been sitting unused for the past ten or twelve years, long after the last train had delivered its final boxcars to a warehouse on the outskirts of town.

Excited, Robbie was convinced this would be his safest option. He pedaled east, and before long, caught his first glimpse of the rusty tracks, obscured in places by weeds.

He wrestled his bike through the undergrowth to the tracks, ignoring the sign warning of federal laws and the dire consequences for trespassing.

He pedaled down the center of the tracks, bumping along, and feeling like his teeth were going to rattle out of his head. He got used to the rhythm soon enough and, while it wasn't comfortable, it was a lot faster than walking, and a lot safer than the streets.

Ten minutes later, Robbie saw a crossing up ahead. He slowed down, hopped his bike over the metal track, and rode down the short gravel slope toward the thick brush, which would provide good concealment. He was very close to Katy's location now, so he decided to leave his bike behind and continue on foot, to make sure his bike didn't become a target again. Katy would be on foot as well, so the bike would probably be a hindrance at this point.

Robbie dropped his pack and took out his survival kit, spare jacket, and some other items, replacing them with some of the additional first aid supplies from his bike's panniers. He made sure to include extra gauze, roller bandage, a small bottle of sterile saline solution, iodine, a pressure bandage and some antibiotic ointment. Then he zipped his panniers shut and pushed the bike behind a large bush. He locked the wheels to the frame again, pulled branches from some nearby bushes and positioned them around the bike. Now it was almost invisible, well camouflaged from prying eyes. Robbie didn't expect anyone to be poking around here, but it was worth the extra couple of minutes to play it safe.

It was time to check in with Katy.

Chapter 33

Katy jumped as the squawk of static filled the room. She flicked on her flashlight and snatched the radio. She quickly turned down the volume and listened closely.

"-you hear me?" The transmission was weak and crackly.

"Robbie, is that you?" she transmitted. She waited. There was no reply. She tried again. Again there was no answer. Frustrated, she stared at the radio, jaw clenched. Suddenly, it burst into life again.

"Katy, can you hear me? It's Robbie. I should be close to your location. Can you hear me now?" The signal was much clearer now. He must have cleared something that had blocked the signal earlier.

"Robbie, I can hear you! But I'm not in the alley anymore. The address I gave your dad is no good. I'm in a building about a block away, around the corner. It's a light brown, four story building. I'm in a janitor's closet. I need water and first aid supplies."

"OK, I'll figure it out, and I have what you need. I'm not far from there, and I can follow the same path you took. We'll have to figure out how I'm going to get in there. Which part of the building are you in?"

"I'm on the third floor, halfway down the hall. The closet door is the one that doesn't have an apartment number on it."

"No wonder your signal was so bad. You probably have concrete and rebar in the way." Robbie paused for a moment. "What's the best way for me to get in? Or can you come down?"

"No, I'm kind of trapped in here. I went in through the front, but I think there might still be guys hanging around who are looking for trouble, and me. Avoid the front. You'd stick out like a sore thumb. Try to find a side or back door."

"OK, I'll scout around and do my best," Robbie replied. "Is the door to the janitor's closet locked?"

"Yes, but if someone wanted to they could kick it down. And if the guys I fought earlier knew I was in here, they'd break it down in a second. That's why you can't let them see you."

"OK. How about I knock four times, quietly? I'll do two quick knocks, a pause and two more quick knocks. And I'll have to sign off in a second, so nobody sees me with the radio. I know it would attract attention around here."

"Sounds good," Katy said. "I'll be here. I've got nowhere else to go."

"Leave your radio on, but don't bother transmitting. Mine will be off for a few minutes when I head in. But I'll want to be able to reach you right away if something comes up."

"OK."

"And I'm going to make sure my dad heard this. We're all on the same frequency." Robbie keyed his radio and called for Jeff, but there was no answer. He must have been out of range. While handheld radios were very useful, a city full of hills, valleys, and occasional tall buildings made getting a clear signal challenging. That would also explain why his dad didn't have an update from Katy. Her signal probably couldn't reach much past where Robbie was.

Robbie hesitated. Katy was trapped and people were looking for her. That sounded dangerous. But they weren't looking for him. They wouldn't know who he was. However, his parents had been clear about staying safe. Walking into this possible hornet's nest was definitely not the safest option. Would he be breaking his promise by going in after her? What would his father do? That was easy. He would try to help Katy, Robbie thought, so that's what he was going to do.

"Katy, I can't reach my dad. We're on our own for now. I'll shut of my radio in a second and head in."

"All right. See you soon. Monitoring."

Robbie turned his radio off and stuffed it in his pack. He was going in.

Chapter 34

Robbie stood up and tightened his backpack straps. He walked down the railroad tracks toward the crossing, staying close to the brush that bordered the tracks. East of the crossing, the tracks weren't on railroad-owned property. Instead, they ran on the pavement, flush with the street surface.

Feeling conspicuous, Robbie thought about how he would look to the locals. He stopped before moving out to the street. He pulled the hood of his sweatshirt over his head, using one of the oldest tricks in the urban camouflage book. Then he fished around in the nearby bushes and found a solid stick, about three feet long. It wasn't as useful as a crowbar or bat for looting or fighting, but it did look the part. Now he looked more like someone intent on breaking windows.

Stick in hand and face partially obscured by his hood, Robbie stepped through the light brush onto the sidewalk and toward the building Katy had described earlier.

Two young men walked in the opposite direction and gave him a quick once-over. Robbie deliberately kept his gaze forward, pretending to ignore them. When he saw they didn't slow down, his confidence level rose and he resisted the urge to walk faster.

Several minutes later, Robbie walked past what he thought was the right building, glancing casually at the group of men out front, on the stoop. One of them shouted something unintelligible at him, but Robbie ignored him and kept walking. Half a dozen empty liquor bottles lay near them on the porch, and the sidewalk was littered with broken bottles. They'd obviously been drinking, a lot.

One of the men kept looking up and down the street, as if searching for someone. He held what looked like a bag of frozen vegetables against his groin.

Robbie kept walking, but this had to be the place. He turned the corner and headed for the alley that ran along the rear of the building. He scanned the length of the block. It was clear.

Robbie stood at the back of the building. A sign posted on the door read "RESIDENTS ONLY! No trespassing! If you see a trespasser, call 911." He tested the door. It was unlocked. Wishing he could call 911, he opened the door and entered.

The smell in the stairwell was oppressive. With the power outage, the ventilation system hadn't been able to remove the odors of cigarette smoke, stale beer, and other things he didn't want to think about. Robbie wrinkled his nose and prayed the smell wouldn't stick to his clothes.

Robbie pulled his LED flashlight from his pocket and set it to its lowest output level. There was a small amount of light coming from a window in the stairwell, but it wasn't enough to be safe, at least not here. Robbie really wanted to avoid stepping in something gross.

He made his way to the third floor and started walking down the hall, shining his flashlight back and forth along the walls, trying to identify the janitor's closet.

A glass bottle bounced loudly off of the wall, and Robbie froze. He'd inadvertently kicked it. He shone the flashlight down. A sack of garbage that someone had set in the hall was tipped over, its contents dumped across the floor. He hadn't even noticed it.

A door to his right flew open and a middle-aged woman in a dingy, stained frock stood in the dim light, glaring at him.

"Who are you?" she demanded. "And why are you creeping around out here?"

"I came to see if my friend was OK," Robbie answered honestly. It sounded plausible enough.

"Why are you sneaking then?" she asked. "And if you come any closer, I'm gonna scream!"

Robbie stepped backward a step and put his hands up. "Don't worry. I'm just checking on my friend. I'll get going."

The woman squinted, her eyes suspicious. "Where'd you get that flashlight? Gimme that. I need it more than you do," she said, stepping toward him, hand outstretched. Robbie yanked it away, surprised at her gall.

"There are still a ton of them at the hardware store. I just came from there, and there aren't any cops around. You could get a bunch of them if you hurry."

The woman's eyes widened with excitement. "City Hardware?"

"Uh... yeah," Robbie replied. He had no idea what stores were in the area, but that one must be the closest. She spun around. "Arthur!" she yelled into the dank apartment. "We gotta get to the hardware store, now. They still got flashlights and other stuff!" With that, she shuffled back inside and slammed the door behind her.

With a nervous look back at the door, Robbie made his way further down the hall. As he neared the middle, he finally spotted the janitor's closet. Heart pounding, he tapped on the door twice, paused, then tapped two more times.

He heard a lock click, the doorknob turned, and the door opened a crack.

A hand reached out and grabbed him.

"Get in here!"

With a quick yank, he was pulled into the closet.

"Sorry," Katy whispered. She pushed the rags back against the crack at the bottom of the door. "I've been a little freaked out sitting in here. And I feel lousy."

"No problem. We'll fix up your arm and get out of here, right?"

"Yeah." Katy showed him her forearm, still covered with the improvised cloth bandage. "But I'm really thirsty. Tell me you brought water."

Robbie shrugged off his pack, set it down and unzipped it. He reached inside and took out his remaining water bottle, twisted off the cap, and handed it to her. Then he carefully pulled out other supplies: saline, iodine, gauze and bandages.

"This should help."

Katy tried to drink slowly, but couldn't help herself and downed a third of the bottle. She paused to breathe, lowered the bottle, and looked over the supplies.

"Give me the saline and some gauze so I can clean the wound." She gently tugged at the bloody cloth that covered her wound, and sighed with relief when she saw the bleeding had stopped.

Robbie removed the lid from the saline bottle and handed it to her. She stood over the sink and squirted saline solution on the wound.

"Gauze."

Robbie held the package of gauze out to her. Katy took a few squares and dabbed the wound, gently wiping away the remaining dirt.

She picked up the saline, squirted more onto the wound, and winced.

Robbie opened the bottle of povidone-iodine[37] and handed it to her. She slowly poured some into the wound, then onto another stack of gauze, and used the gauze to finish cleaning around the wound. Her jaw clenched as her exposed nerve endings sent alarm signals to her brain. The cut was much more painful now, since the adrenaline in her system had dissipated.

"What kind of bandages do you have?"

Robbie rummaged around and pulled out a sealed, olive green plastic package.

"Perfect," Katy said. She knew what it was: an Israeli military bandage.[38] "Go ahead and open it, but don't touch the white part."

"I know that," Robbie said, giving her an irritated look. "I was there when my dad showed you how to use it."

"Sorry," Katy said, flashing an apologetic smile. "I'll try not to get all bossy with you."

"Don't worry about it," Robbie replied. "Want me to apply it for you? It'll be easier than doing it yourself."

"Go ahead."

Robbie carefully placed the padding over the wound, covering it completely, before winding the bandage's long tail around her arm, making sure to cover both sides of the dressing, and sealing off the wound area. Katy sipped water as she watched. After a few more wraps, he paused.

"How's the pressure?"

"Perfect. Good job."

When finished wrapping, he slipped the tail into a plastic clip over the covered wound area, tying it off.

"All set. What now?"

"I lost quite a bit of blood back there, and got pretty dizzy. I still feel light-headed. I'm concerned my blood pressure might be too low."

"Well, I definitely didn't bring any blood. And I don't have any more water with me," he said, glancing at the empty water bottle. "What about the sink?"

"I don't think so. The water that comes out of that sink looks really bad," Katy said, making a face. "Look for yourself."

Robbie opened the tap. Mud-colored water trickled out.

131

"It's not clean, but it's water," he said. "And you're right. It looks pretty gross. We could use the iodine to disinfect the water," he suggested, rummaging around in his pack, "but we'd have to wait a while for it to be safe. And it would still be brown. I have a better idea." He pulled out a foil bag and a small black cylinder.

"What's that?" Katy asked.

"It's a squeeze filter," he explained. "We fill up this Mylar bag with water, like this." Robbie filled the foil bag at the faucet. "And then we attach the filter piece like this." He screwed on the cylinder, about the size of a candy bar. "Then we fill up your clean water bottle with clean water." He gave the bag a squeeze, and a stream of clean water squirted out, slowly filling the bottle. Katy looked skeptical.

"Are you sure it's safe?"

"Yep. I've used this camping before, in an area where we were warned to purify our water. And I tried it with muddy water too. No problems." He handed her the full bottle.

Katy took a sip. "Aaaah," she sighed contentedly. "Thank you. Tastes great."

"We could also attach that filter to the bottle itself, and drink from the filter directly, but this way we keep your bottle clean, and we can fill the sack back up before we leave."

"Yeah, we need to get going," Katy said, getting to her feet.

"Hold on a minute," Robbie said. "You need to give your body a few minutes to absorb the water. We're not in any immediate danger, right?"

"OK," Katy said as she sat back down. Moments later, the bottle was empty.

Robbie filled the Mylar bag again, then refilled her water bottle.

"How long does the filter last?"

"You can only filter a million gallons[39] before you need to replace it," Robbie said, grinning.

"Are you serious?"

"That's what it said on the box. But I'll never filter enough water to ever test it."

Robbie filled the bag one more time. "Now we'll have more for later." He squirted some into his mouth from the filter, then closed the pop-top on the end, sealing it shut. "This tastes way better than if we'd used the iodine."

"You can use the same stuff I just used to clean my cut?"

"Yep. Iodine kills all kinds of bad stuff. Eight drops per liter, but you have to wait half an hour.[40] I've used it camping. And I've used a pump-type filter too. It was a ton of work, but it did the job. But after my dad got me this squeeze filter, I never went back."

Katy looked impressed.

"Hey, are you hungry? I have an MRE for you if you want it," Robbie offered.

"No thanks. I've been sick to my stomach. I don't think I could keep it down." She rubbed her stomach. "I think I'll be OK to walk more after I get some more water into me, but I don't know how far I'll be able to run. I'm feeling a little bit better now, but I'm not feeling back to normal yet. By the way, how did you get in here without getting spotted?"

"I came in the back. We're not dealing with an organized group here," Robbie said. "And they weren't looking for a boy coming in anyhow. I did see some guys out front, and they looked pretty unhappy." He gave Katy an appraising look. "One of them had an icepack on his crotch." It was more of a question than a statement.

"Yeah, that's one of them," Katy said with a scowl. "If they knew I was in there, they would have already broken down the door, even if they had to beat it open with their heads. I really ticked them off. I bet the other one is still out there looking for me." Her scowl turned to a tight grin as she imagined the jerk on the porch, holding his groin.

133

"We'll go out the back door," Robbie said. "Do they think you're still in here?"

"I don't know. Probably not. But this is the last place they know I've been." Katy explained her ruse with the bloody handprints. It was Robbie's turn to look impressed.

"You have a map, right?" she asked.

"I have lots of great stuff in my backpack." For a moment, he felt like he was in one of his favorite X-Box games, running around fighting bad guys, collecting different weapons, power-ups and loot, and putting them in the character's backpack. A pack full of loot was a wonderful thing.[41]

Robbie unfolded the street map and pointed to a spot inside a large penciled circle. "We're here."

"Which way did you come here? And what do you think is the best way back?"

"I came this way," Robbie said, tracing the path he'd taken. "But we don't want to go back that way. I had my own run-in."

"What happened? Are you OK?" Katy asked in surprise, feeling a little guilty that she'd been so focused on her own problems.

"Yeah, I'm fine, but I was worried." He briefly described the encounter with the boys by the water tower.

"Wow, glad you're all right." Katy paused for moment, marveling at how crazy their situation had become.

"Are you about ready to go?" Robbie asked. "I think it's time to get moving." He put the water in his pack. "You can hold onto the map if you want."

"I feel better." Katy folded it up and put it in her pocket.

"We'll go out the back, and then we can go east to 140th before cutting over to 16th. What should we do if we get separated?"

"We won't," Katy promised, and then hesitated. "I guess it won't hurt to have a plan, just in case. How about we meet at the intersection of 130th and 8th, and we'll make sure our radios are on with volumes up if we're separated."

Robbie looked at his watch again.

"Uh oh. Speaking of radios, Mom and Dad will definitely be freaking out by now. We need to make contact as soon as we can."

"Well, it's not going to work from here, so let's get going."

They turned off their flashlights and the closet was plunged into darkness. Robbie stood in front of the door, but didn't move.

"What are you waiting for?" Katy whispered impatiently.

"Letting my eyes adjust for a second. I'd like to avoid using our lights as much as possible in the hallway. I don't want to attract attention."

"We're fine. Let's go."

"Wait a sec," Robbie said. "Sorry, I thought of something else." Robbie fumbled around in the dark. "Here. Take this and put it on. It's my hoodie. They'll have a tougher time recognizing you in this. Put the hood up and it'll hide your hair."

"Good idea."

"OK." Robbie opened the door and popped his head out. The hallway was empty. Katy let the door close behind them with a quiet click, and they tiptoed toward the rear stairwell.

Chapter 35

They walked carefully down the rear stairwell without seeing a soul, and exited the building into bright sunshine and cool, fresh air. They stood, blinking at the top of the concrete steps. Katy sneezed.

"Go," Robbie said, and they moved out, back to the street. At the end of the block they turned left. An old woman sitting on the front steps of the building across the street scowled at them, but the street was otherwise deserted.

"Lucky us," Katy said. "Everyone must be out pillaging."

They walked three blocks east, the last two uphill, leaving the last of the apartment buildings behind. This neighborhood was made up of small houses, and felt less intimidating. Even the occasional sight of a burned-out shell didn't dampen their spirits. They each felt as if a weight had been lifted from their shoulders. Things were getting better, and they had officially exited North Lake.

Unlike the apartment buildings they left behind, in this area nearly every house had broken windows and other damage. In the space of two blocks, two houses had slid completely off their foundations, three had caved in, and three others had collapsed carports. These houses appeared decades older, and most of them probably hadn't been upgraded to modern earthquake standards.

"Do you think we can check in now?" Katy asked, as she looked past Robbie as some people clearing rubble out of their yard. Robbie looked back down the way they'd come and nodded.

"Yeah, we're up a bit higher now, and away from those tall buildings. Let's give it a try." They stepped into the shade of an oak that overhung the sidewalk and Robbie pulled his radio from his pack.

"Dad, are you there? NM8J, this is KE7CTA," he added. He'd barely finished when Jeff's voice burst through the radio.

"Robbie! Where are you? Are you OK? Fill me in!"

"We're at the corner of Southeast 2nd and 142nd. Katy's a little weak and dehydrated, but she's had some water, her cut is bandaged, and she's feeling a little better. Nobody's bothering us. I had to leave my bike in some bushes near the railroad tracks, but the wheels are locked and it's pretty well hidden."

"I have good news. We found a route. If you can get to Southeast 4th and 150th," Jeff said, "we can pick you up. We cleared one of the downed trees in our neighborhood, and it looks like we can get that far with no problem."

"Uh, there may be one small problem," Robbie confessed hesitantly. "The guys that hurt Katy are hunting for her. And some boys I pepper-sprayed might be looking for me too."

There was a long pause.

"You can tell me the story later. I want you to move as quickly as you can," Jeff instructed. There was an edge in his voice that hadn't been there moments before. Here's where we'll meet," he added, describing the area. "We'll be there in a few minutes. You get there as fast as you can. I'm going to round up some people to help. Can you run?"

"No. Katy lost a lot of blood. She gets dizzy if we walk too fast."

"Well, walk as fast as you can, and let me know each time you cross an intersection. Leave your radio on. I'll track your progress as you go, and I'll let you know how close we are."

They were all in a race now, but didn't know it.

Chapter 36

Katy and Robbie kept up a brisk pace, updating Jeff regularly. Occasionally, a car would pass. These streets weren't clogged with car wrecks, rubble, or downed trees like some of the others they'd seen. An Oldsmobile went by, driven by an older man who had both hands on the wheel and stared straight ahead. Another car went by in the opposite direction, stuffed with two adults in front and two kids in the back. Plastic bags of stuff obscured the back window, and several suitcases were tied to the roof.

They kept walking at a good pace. The water had definitely helped Katy regain some of her energy. Not much longer and they'd be home free.

A dark green sedan approached at a leisurely pace. It slowed down even more as it passed, and the two men inside stared at Katy. The man on the passenger side pointed at them, talking to the driver excitedly.

The car made a quick U-turn, tires squealing, and sped back down the hill. Katy and Robbie looked at each other.

"Do you think they recognized me?" Katy asked.

"Yes," Robbie answered.

"They must be going to get reinforcements," Katy said with a frown. "This is bad. We need to get off this road."

Robbie glanced at her arm.

"Can you go faster?"

"I'll have to. Let's go."

Katy started jogging, and Robbie followed. They turned right, jogged a block and turned left. Katy's pace was slowing.

"Hold on!" Katy gasped. She bent over, hands on her knees, trying to catch her breath. "I guess I'm not ready to run yet."

"Can you at least walk?" Robbie said. "We really need to get farther away from where they saw us."

Katy didn't reply, saving her energy. But she did start walking again, following Robbie and breathing rapidly.

"Water," Katy said between gasps.

Robbie slowed, pulled the bottle out of his pack and handed it to Katy.

"Keep moving."

She took a long drink and started walking again. They covered two more blocks at a slow but steady pace.

"I need a break," Katy protested, panting heavily. Robbie gently guided her toward some bushes at the next corner, in front of a partially collapsed house.

"Get behind those," he urged. "And I'll take a quick look." Ducking down with her, he took off his backpack and felt around for his binoculars.

Robbie peered down the hill. Movement caught his eye two blocks away. A red truck sat idling in front of a house. The driver was talking to a man in the front yard. The man pointed up the hill toward them. At that moment, he spotted the green sedan a block away as it crossed the intersection, heading uphill.

"Go! Hide now," Robbie cried, backing away from the bush they'd been using as cover. They ran toward the house, darting through the side gate and into the backyard. He peeked around the corner in time to see the red truck crawling by. One of the occupants had a large white bandage on his cheek.

"Let's sit tight and see if they come back," Robbie suggested.

Katy nodded, her face ashen. She sipped more water, trying to rehydrate. Minutes later, the truck drove by in the opposite direction, faster this time.

Robbie crept forward to the bushes and saw the truck heading down the hill. At the bottom sat the green sedan. The two vehicles pulled up alongside each other and Robbie saw the driver of the truck point back up the hill.

Robbie ducked out of view and scurried back behind the house.

"NM8J, this is KE7CTA," he hissed into his radio. "We're near 145th and 3rd. There are two vehicles looking for us, a red truck and a green sedan. They have a good idea where we are. Katy's winded and we can't run. Can you drive here?"

"Stay with the current plan," Jeff said. "I can't find a way to get to 145th yet. There are trees and power poles down all over the place, and we keep having to detour. But we're close to the rendezvous point. A few more blocks and you should see us. We'll drive as far as we can, then head out on foot if you're not there yet."

"Will do, Dad. I'll leave my radio on."

Katy and Robbie opened the gate and walked away from the house. They quickly walked down the sidewalk to the south, toward Southeast Fourth. The area looked familiar. Then Robbie recognized the house they passed. He'd ridden his bike here earlier.

"I came through here on my way in."

They ducked behind a bush again as they heard a car coming back up the hill. Robbie looked across the street and did a double-take when he saw the girl he'd given water to earlier that morning. She was sitting on the porch again and watching them curiously. As their eyes met, she waved.

Robbie didn't move, waiting for the vehicle to pass. The green sedan cruised by, then turned the corner without spotting them. It looked like it was doing a grid search of the area. When it disappeared, Robbie listened for the truck. He couldn't hear it.

"Wait here a minute," he said to Katy. "I'll be right back." He dashed across the street.

"Hi!" the girl said as he approached.

"Can you help us? There are some guys in a red truck and a green car, the car that just passed. They tried to hurt my friend earlier, but she got away, and I'm trying to get her home. We're in big trouble if they find us. If they ask, can you tell them we went that way?" he asked, pointing up the nearby alley heading in the opposite direction.

"Sure," the girl said, sitting up. "Do you need a place to hide? You can use our yard. My folks are taking a nap. They won't care."

"That'd be great. It'll just be until these guys start looking somewhere else. We're supposed to meet my dad near here."

Robbie waved Katy over. The girl scampered down the steps and led them around the side of the house, where they concealed themselves behind some garbage cans.

"They won't be able to see you here," she said, and ran back around to the front.

As Katy drank the last of her water bottle, they heard the growl of an engine, and the screech of brakes as a car stopped in front of the house. They pressed themselves against the back of the house and listened. They couldn't make out what was being said, but Robbie could hear the girl's voice. Then there was the sound of another vehicle, and doors slamming shut. Robbie threw Katy an anxious glance and turned down the radio's volume, hoping his dad wouldn't choose this time to call them.

Doors slammed again, followed by screeching tires. The engine sounds faded away. It sounded like they were driving down the alley Robbie had pointed out earlier. He poked his head around the side of the house in time to see the car and truck both turn down the alley and speed out of view. He sagged against the house in relief.

The girl turned around and spotted him. She gave him a toothy grin and a thumbs up.

Robbie gave her a wave and ducked back behind the house, rejoining Katy. He keyed his radio.

"Dad, the car and the truck are driving down an alley, away from us. We're heading your way."

"OK. We're still on the move, but should be at the rendezvous point in a couple minutes. Hurry up and stay safe."

The girl appeared, still grinning, clearly enjoying her role in the deception.

"I told them I saw a boy with a backpack and a lady with a hoodie running into the alley and they took off. They didn't even say thank you." She rolled her eyes. "Rude." She grinned again.

"Thanks," Robbie said.

"That was brave of you," Katy said. "Now you better go back inside for a while. Lock your door and don't answer it. They might come back, and they're no good. You don't want to talk to them again."

"OK," she said. "By the way, I'm Teera. Who are you?"

"I'm Robbie, and this is Katy."

"Nice to meet you both," she said. "Good luck."

Chapter 37

Jeff drove down the hill as fast as he could while still scanning for downed power lines or other hazards. Peter sat in the back, behind Jeff, keeping an eye out his window, while Jackson did the same from the front passenger seat.

They crested a small rise and had a clear view ahead. A tree lay across the road several hundred yards up, a car crushed beneath it. The rest of the road was empty. Jeff braked and came to a stop in the center of the intersection.

Jackson pressed his binoculars to his eyes, scanning. There wasn't a soul in sight. He swiveled slightly, as movement caught his eye.

"There's the red truck," he said, pointing without lowering the binoculars. "It just crossed, a couple blocks down that way. I don't see Robbie or Katy, but I don't think they've been spotted, because the truck was moving slowly."

At that moment, Peter saw Robbie and Katy emerge from a side street and run toward them.

"There they are!" Jeff and Peter said, simultaneously.

"We see you, Robbie," Jeff said, into his radio, stomping on the gas and flying down the hill, toward the downed tree. "We're on the other side of the tree, coming down the hill."

Robbie reached for the radio on his belt and raised it to his mouth. Jeff's radio crackled.

"We see you, Dad. We're headed toward you!"

"Be careful. The red truck is around. It just crossed a block below you, a few seconds ago."

"We'll stay to one side and keep out of sight," Robbie replied.

Robbie and Katy were a little over two hundred yards away from the downed tree when the green sedan shot out of a side road, several blocks behind them. Tires shrieked as it careened around the corner, and its engine revved as it accelerated toward them.

"They see you!" Jeff shouted into his radio, as the truck skidded to a stop in front of the tree. "Get up here now!"

Katy and Robbie broke into a run, moving as fast as their weary legs could take them.

The green car was bearing down on them. There was another squeal of tires and the red truck appeared, taking the corner hard and falling in behind the green car. Then an arm snaked out of the passenger window of the green car. A shot rang out.

Katy and Robbie instantly veered right at the next corner, knowing there was no way to reach Jeff before being run down by their pursuers. After just a few yards, they dove to the ground behind the first concealment they saw, a low hedge bordering a park.

"What the heck! Why are they shooting?" Robbie gasped. "What did you do to them?"

"All I did was fight them off when they attacked me!" Katy hissed back, panting. "They're crazy!"

"This is bad," Robbie said, panic rising. "Really, really bad."

"Think!" Katy urged. "There has to be a way out of here. Where should we go now?"

Then they heard a thumping sound behind them. They turned around quickly, and to their horror, they saw a tall man with a grim expression on his face, running straight toward them from the center of the park.

They were trapped.

145

Chapter 38

For the last half hour, Neil had been monitoring Jeff and Robbie's conversation, after locking his scanner[42] onto their frequency. The signal was clear, which meant they weren't far away. Just a couple of minutes earlier, he had stopped briefly to check the street names that the voices had been referencing, and it looked like they were in the same neighborhood now. He kept to his northbound route, wondering whether they would cross paths. It seemed unlikely.

A red truck turned the corner ahead, driving toward Neil. When the driver caught sight of Neil, the truck slowed. Its two occupants looked him up and down as it got closer. Then as it passed, the passenger locked eyes with Neil, made the shape of a gun with his hand, index finger extended, and pointed it at him, pretending to shoot. Neil stopped, eyes narrowed, and turned to watch the truck speed around the next corner. Based on the radio conversation he'd overheard, Neil had a good idea who they were, and he got a sinking feeling in his stomach as he started playing out potential scenarios.

He wasn't interested in getting involved in someone else's emergency, but from the desperation he could hear in these people's voices, they really needed help. Troublemakers rarely sought help, especially on ham radio frequencies, and the two guys he just saw had to be one group of pursuers he'd heard about earlier.

He looked around actively, trying to spot two people on the run. The roads were empty, making it easier to see any movement. They must be nearby, he thought. He reached the next intersection, and looked around. There was a small park about a hundred yards ahead.

Aside from a few climbing toys and a small basketball court, it was a flat, open expanse that would provide a better view than his current position. As he headed toward it, he turned up the scanner's volume, listening with growing concern as the conversation unfolded.

"Get up here now!"

At the sound of the voice from his scanner, Neil made up his mind. Renee would understand. He committed. He was going to help. Then he heard the unmistakable sound of gunfire, only a few blocks away.

Neil's heart raced. Striding briskly toward the park, he clipped the scanner to a piece of webbing on the side of the pack and cinched the straps down even more tightly, for greater stability. He broke into a jog, feeling his leg muscles burn with the increased effort. The nearly nonstop walking over the past day had consumed much of his energy reserves. He was probably burning muscle for fuel now, instead of fat, but he didn't care. He had a new job to do.

Breathing heavily, legs pumping painfully, Neil picked up the pace and ran. Reaching the park, he burst headlong into the open grassy area and looked around. It was time to turn on his radio and let the people know he was going to help. He cursed under his breath, realizing he should have done that a long time ago. He started to unsling his pack to retrieve his radio, when movement to his right caught his eye.

He turned and spotted two figures running down the street on the other side of the park. They leapt over the bushes lining the sidewalk and flattened themselves on the ground. Nobody else was in sight.

Neil knew who they were.

The two were talking in hushed tones, focused on the road on the other side of the hedge. But it didn't take long for them to hear Neil as he rapidly closed in. As they turned and saw him, their eyes widened with fear.

Chapter 39

"Shut up and stay down!" the man hissed at the startled couple, as he dropped to the ground beside them. "You must be the boy on the radio," he gasped, trying to catch his breath.

"Who are you? What are you doing here?" Katy demanded.

"I heard you talking on my scanner," Neil replied, pointing to his pack. "There wasn't time to get my radio to tell you. It sounded like you could use some help. And I saw a red truck cruising around, looking for someone. Didn't take a genius to figure they were looking for you. Fill me in."

Robbie and Katy looked at each other. They didn't need to say anything. It was obvious that this man was one of the good guys.

"I'm Robbie. This is Katy. My dad's just up that way," Robbie said, pointing east. "We saw him but the road was blocked. He and his friends came to get us."

"I'm Neil. Sorry to meet you like this. Where did you see the car or truck last?"

"They were coming up the hill behind us."

As if on cue, an engine roared as a vehicle turned the corner and sped past the park. The car and truck were closing in.

Jeff's voice burst from Neil's scanner and Robbie's radio simultaneously, startling them.

"Robbie, are you OK? Talk to me!"

149

Neil quickly turned his scanner's volume down, not wanting the sound to give away their position.

Robbie turned his radio's volume down too, then transmitted quietly.

"Dad, we're at a park a couple blocks down the hill and around the corner. We just heard one of them pass. And we met a guy named Neil who wants to help."

"We need to move," Neil interrupted. "Now."

"Hold on a sec, Dad. We have to move."

Katy nodded. "Let's go."

"Follow me." Neil started jogging back the way he'd come, ignoring the pain in his exhausted legs. He threw a quick glance over his shoulder as they crossed a street, to ensure the pair were keeping up.

Half a block from the park, they heard another vehicle approaching.

"Get down," Neil hissed. "Here!" He dove over a three-foot hedge in front of a house and dropped prone on the other side. The others quickly followed. Robbie landed on top of Neil and they both grunted.

"Sorry," Robbie said, rolling off him.

"Shh! Don't move!" They listened as a car, engine rumbling, crept toward them like a lion on the prowl. They all held their breath as it continued past them, down the block.

Robbie looked around and then sat up, his back against the hedge. He looked at Neil.

"So what are you doing here?"

"I'm just trying to walk home. Heard you on the scanner. You know the rest. And you?"

"Robbie and I are neighbors," Katy said. "I got caught in the quake downtown. Robbie and his dad were trying to help me get home. It's been a rough day."

"OK guys, here's the deal. I was listening to ham frequencies to learn what I could about the area, when I came across yours.

When you described your position, I realized I was close by. I kept listening and figured you were in trouble. I'll help you."

"Nice gun," Katy asked, pointing to his waistband. His shirt was riding up, exposing the holster and the butt of his pistol.

"Don't freak out. I'm a good guy, and licensed to carry."

"I was actually hoping you had a spare" she said. "I left mine at home." Her right arm was still throbbing, but she was sure she could still manage to shoot a handgun.

"Sorry." Neil shook his head, a curious look on his face. They froze as they heard another vehicle approach from the opposite direction. It passed, tires slowly crunching bits of loose gravel.

"They're not giving up," he said in a whisper. "They know you're here, somewhere. If we stay here, it's only a matter of time before they find us. They might not see us through the hedge, but we're still too exposed. We have to keep moving."

"Robbie, tell me what's going on!" Jeff demanded over the radio. Even with the volume low, Robbie could tell his father was upset.

"Dad, we're hiding again for a minute," Robbie said as he got to his knees, preparing to move again.

"Tell him we're going to circle the block that way," Neil said, as he made a motion south and east. Then he pulled out his smartphone and accessed the GPS application.

Robbie tersely relayed the information.

Neil's phone locked onto the GPS satellites and a small black circle appeared on the map. With a flick of his fingers, he zoomed in.

"This is where we are." They huddled over the small screen.

Robbie's radio crackled again.

"Circling the block should be fine," Jeff said. "And who the heck is Neil?"

Robbie glanced at Neil, who stuck out his hand. Robbie handed him the radio.

"Hi, this is Neil, K9NEL[43]. I'm trying to help your son and his friend. You're Robbie's dad?"

"Yeah, I'm Jeff." There was a brief pause. "Thanks for your help."

"No problem. If you're going to be on foot, it'll take at least a few minutes for you to reach our position. These guys are armed and in a car. They've been back and forth near our location and are probably still close." He paused for a moment, thinking, and released the transmit button in case Jeff wanted to say something.[44]

"Do you have any better ideas?" Jeff asked.

Neil looked at the map on his phone again.

"If we go east on 4th, I think it'll be safer. It looks like there are several approaches we can take at that point, with parallel roads heading east on either side. We could connect on any of them. Sound good?"

"Yeah." They agreed on an intersection. So far, any plans they made didn't survive long. But the location gave them a common starting point.[45]

"I'll be monitoring,[46]" Jeff said. "See you soon."

"Are you a ham, too?" Robbie asked Neil, as they got ready to move.

"Yeah. For a long time. We can talk about this later. Let's get moving." They set off, heading toward 4th.

Chapter 40

After a brisk hike three blocks south, the group turned left, and started following the road uphill. They should connect with Jeff in just a few more blocks, according to Neil's map.

An engine roared a few blocks ahead of them, but it didn't belong to a car or truck. It sounded like a small motorcycle. It was followed by a massive, thumping crash.

"Dad, did you hear that?" Robbie called softly into the radio, out of breath from the pace they'd been maintaining. There was a brief pause before he heard his dad's voice.

"That was me. I cut down a tree to block the road. When we pick you up, I don't want anyone following us out of here."

So it been a chainsaw.

"Your dad's on the ball," Neil said, looking at Robbie.

Robbie grinned with pride and kept walking.

"Where are you?" Jeff asked impatiently. "You should be here by now."

Neil motioned for Robbie's radio again.

"We're still a few blocks away, just a couple north and another couple west, from the sound of that tree falling."

"Hurry up. We're ready to take you out of here. We don't see any cars on the road."

"OK," Robbie panted. They broke from a brisk walk into a jog, despite their exhaustion. They were all determined to end the nightmare they'd found themselves in.

They jogged past a run-down rambler. A wiry man in a dirty t-shirt sat on the front porch, scowling at them as they passed. He held a radio up to his mouth and spoke loud enough for them to hear.

"This is Smitty. Got 'em. They're here, right in front of my house."

They heard a muttered reply emit from the radio, "...coming," but the rest was inaudible.

"That's great," Neil huffed. "The bad guys have radios. Who did you pick a fight with, anyway?" Neil asked between breaths. "Looks like they're connected."

"They picked the fight," Katy growled back. "And they're scumbags."

Neil glanced around, but didn't see anything or hear any cars. The man continued to glare at them as they jogged away, talking into his radio again.

"That looks like my FRS[47] radio," Katy continued, frustrated. "Those things are everywhere. If I hadn't lost the stuff in my pack, we could have used my radio to hear what they're saying."

Robbie updated his dad without breaking stride, and between breaths, asked him to scan the FRS/GMRS frequencies.

"Keep it up!" Neil urged. "We're out of time." Two minutes before, he'd been sure they'd escaped danger. Now, he wasn't sure of anything.

They continued along the side street, heading northward toward the next intersection, where they would turn right, up the hill to Jeff and, hopefully, safety.

"Robbie," Jeff's voice crackled, "I just heard someone say that they're almost there. Do you see anyone?"

"No," he panted, "but we're almost to your location."

"Don't let up," Neil ordered, chest heaving. Nobody had breath to reply.

When the trio rounded the next corner, they spotted Jeff and his friends about two hundred yards east, up the hill.

"I see you," Robbie's radio chirped. "Hurry up!"

Tires squealed behind them. They all threw anxious looks behind them as they ran. The green car was three blocks farther down the hill and closing fast. The street was straight, running west to east, and gave everyone a clear view, which was both an advantage and a disadvantage. Everyone could see everyone, but Neil hoped that the car's occupants would be so intent on their prey that they would fail to notice Jeff and his friends further on.

As the car closed in, only two blocks behind the three runners, the passenger in the green sedan reached out the window once again and started shooting.

Chapter 41

A moment later, the truck roared out from a side street and pulled alongside the green car, joining the chase.

Peter and Jackson were ready. With no hesitation, their shotguns snapped up and thunderous gunshots roared, making the thugs' handgun sound like a toy.

Peter and Jackson were both firing 12-gauge, double-ought buckshot rounds and they were both experienced trap shooters,[48] so they had no problem tracking these targets.

The car and truck roared forward, unaffected. Only a few pellets reached them, and the rest skipped along the empty street.[49] While it was mostly a waste of ammunition due to the long range, Peter and Jackson had hoped to at least disable the vehicles. But they didn't even slow down.

Jeff realized far too late that he shouldn't have created the roadblock. It would stop anyone following them, but it had also effectively trapped his truck. Now he needed to move on foot. As his friends started firing, Jeff started running, parallel with the field of fire and toward Robbie and the others. With a storm of lead flying to his right, he sprinted downhill, carrying his rifle in both hands, and keeping his eyes locked on the two approaching vehicles.

The results of the shotgun fire were unimpressive at first. But as the car and truck sped toward the group, the barrage became more and more accurate. Several pellets impacted their windshields. But instead of veering away, both vehicles picked up speed. The red truck slowed momentarily and pulled behind the green car, but from the higher elevation, the two shotgun-wielding marksmen still had clear views of both targets.

Robbie and Katy were on the ground now, crawling for cover away from the road, but Neil had taken several steps down the hill. He stood with his pistol straight out in front of him at eye level, in a two-handed grip. He rapidly fired his entire seven-round magazine. He shot four times at the car, then three at the truck. He was fast. In a flash, he reloaded from a spare magazine on his belt, and fired three more shots at the car. One of the tires burst.

The green car swerved, then screeched to a halt, only thirty yards from Robbie, Katy, and Neil. The truck slammed into the back of the car, then both vehicles slid farther, brakes screeching. Then there was silence.

Jeff was still sprinting, only twenty yards away from Robbie and Katy.

Robbie craned his head from behind a low shrub to get a better look. It was clear now that the shotguns had taken their toll. He could see multiple holes in the grill and windshields of both vehicles, and the car had a flat tire on the front passenger side.

Starter motors ground away, but neither engine started. Seconds later, men spilled out and fell to the ground. Three of them appeared to be injured by shotgun pellets or broken glass, but were able to stand up quickly. And all but one raised their empty hands high, all shouting variations of "I give up! Don't shoot me!"

But the car's passenger, who had been firing out the window earlier, still held his gun in his hand as he got out. He sported a blood-spotted bandage on one cheek.

Katy saw it was Rodney.

Jeff instantly dropped to a knee, simultaneously shouldering his rifle.

While he knew a laser wasn't the most important accessory to put on a rifle, the flashlight he had attached to the fore-stock had come with one built in. The laser dot was clearly visible even in bright daylight, and now it bounced up and down rhythmically, in time with Jeff's heavy breathing. To round out his sight picture, the Aimpoint[50] red-dot sight he'd mounted on the top of the rifle lined up perfectly with the laser dot centered on Rodney's chest, allowing Jeff to keep both eyes open while keeping the rifle on target.

"Drop the gun! Do it now or I shoot!" Jeff shouted. "Trust me," he added, "I really, really want to shoot you right now."

Rodney looked down, hypnotized by the red dot bouncing on his chest. He opened his hand and dropped the gun, without looking up. It clattered to the ground.

"Get on your knees, now!"

Rodney kneeled, still staring down at his chest.

"Lay on your face and put your hands out in front of you on the ground! Cross your ankles!"

Rodney complied.

"That's one of the guys who attacked me," Katy shouted, popping up. She was peering over nearby bushes, where she'd been anxiously watching the events unfold.

"Who else?" Jeff asked.

"I don't see the other one."

Keeping his rifle aimed at Rodney, Jeff turned slightly toward the other men who were still standing with hands held high.

Neil took several steps forward, his pistol trained on the group. Peter and Jackson had closed in by now as well, and took positions behind Jeff, shotguns trained on the group.

"The rest of you, lift your shirts and turn around!"

They all lifted their shirts and turned around slowly, showing their waistbands. They all had chains extending from their belt loops to their back pockets, securing their wallets, but it was clear they weren't carrying any handguns. Miraculously, other than a couple of minor cuts, all of them appeared to be uninjured.

"All of you get on your knees and keep your hands up."

They kneeled, awkwardly, trying to keep their hands as high as possible.

"Don't move, or we start shooting, and at this distance we can't miss," Jeff said to the group.

He took a quick look around, then motioned with his head for Neil to join him and his friends.

"What do we do with them?" Jeff asked in a low voice. "The shooter has to go down, but I don't want to mess with all of them. And I doubt I could convince what's left of the police department to do anything with them."

"Pepper spray them and let them go," Peter suggested. "They won't bother anyone for a while, and then they'll have UV dye[51] on them, in case the police decide they're interested later."

"That's a good idea," Neil said, "but you should do more to make sure they're not a problem in the future. Take their IDs. You can give them to the cops later, if you want. And I can take their pictures with my phone. That should get them thinking."

"I like it," Jackson said. Peter nodded.

"Done," Jeff replied. "Neil, are you OK getting their IDs?"

"Sure."

Peter and Jackson changed position to cover the group from each side as Neil walked over. He holstered his pistol and retrieved a knife from the other side of his waistband. The blade glinted the light as he reached toward the first man.

"Hey, what are you doing?" the man demanded.

"Shut up, or I might slip and accidentally cut you," Neil threatened. The man was silent.

Neil cut through the man's belt loop, pulled his wallet out by its chain, and took his picture, then repeated the process with each of them. With a handful of chains and dangling wallets, Neil stepped back to get everyone in view.

"Smile," he said as he took a group picture. Nobody smiled. "All set," he told the others.

"My turn," Jackson said, slinging his shotgun as he approached the punks. Neil had his handgun out again, pointed at the group, and they were all looking uncomfortably back and forth from the pistol to the shotgun.

"Don't worry," Jackson said. "You'll be free to go in a minute."

Before they were able to figure out what he meant, Jackson swept his pepper spray fogger across the group. While some of them were able to duck before he got to them, that only ensured he spent extra time coating their heads before letting up.

Jeff shouted over their curses. "We know who you are. Don't ever come back here. If you come back here, we will shoot you. You won't get another warning. We won't be nice to you like we were this time. Now get out of here!"

They all started stumbling down the hill, coughing and clutching their faces.

Rodney didn't move.

Jackson and Peter turned their shotguns and took two more shots each at the vehicles' engine compartments. The fleeing men picked up their pace.

Jeff walked toward Rodney with slow, measured steps, stopping three yards away, rifle trained on his torso.

"Cover me," Jeff said to Jackson. Rodney's eyes widened as he turned to see the smoking shotgun barrel aimed at his face.

"Hands behind your back, now," Jeff growled.

Rodney complied immediately.

Jeff pulled a zip-tie from a pocket, and quickly cinched it tight across Rodney's wrists. Then he pulled out a second one and repeated the process. "We're going for a little ride." He yanked upward, forcing Rodney to his feet. "Jackson, please search this scumbag, then duct tape him and toss him in the back of the truck. We have a quick stop to make on our way home. After yesterday, I know where we can drop him. The police won't be happy to see me again so soon, but they will be happy this piece of filth is off the street."

"He might have a knife like the other guy," Katy said. "Check his waistband."

Rodney stayed silent, scowling, but not daring to look up at Katy.

As Jackson got to work, Jeff finally looked over toward Robbie and Katy, who were still standing behind the bushes lining the sidewalk. He lowered his rifle and let it hang from its sling.

"Dad!" Robbie yelled, and tumbled over the hedge. He ran over and threw himself into his father's arms.

"I'm glad you're safe, Robbie," Jeff said, and hugged him tightly. After a moment, he said "Now we need to get you home before your mom kills me."

Robbie gave Jeff another squeeze, then Katy took a turn.

"Thank you, Jeff," she said, her voice breaking slightly.

"You're welcome. Let's get out of here," Jeff said.

Jackson held up Rodney's knife. Jeff and Jackson looked at Katy.

"Tires?" Jeff asked with a grin.

"My pleasure," Katy replied. She retrieved the knife and methodically slashed the tires on both vehicles. It felt good.

Peter retrieved Rodney's dropped handgun and secured it in his waistband. Then he searched the vehicles' glove boxes for any owner documentation, for the police to use later.

Jeff turned to Neil. "Neil, thank you. I owe you one."

"No problem," Neil replied. "I was in the neighborhood, and I had to help."

"I really can't thank you enough. What can I do for you? Do you need anything? Where are you headed?"

"North of Kirkland," Neil said, "where my wife is waiting for me."

"The roads are all blocked that way from what I've heard so far, or I'd give you a ride. Can I give you any supplies? Water? We have some stuff in the truck. Anything you need – it's yours."

"You wouldn't happen to have a couple of MREs to go with the water, would you? Oh, and do you have any extra .45 ammo? I used up a lot of mine. I hope I won't need any more, but you never know."

Jeff started thumbing cartridges out of one of his pistol magazines, while Robbie retrieved the food and water from the truck.

"There's something else. Any chance you could monitor that frequency for a while?" Neil asked. "I could use a little conversation, as long as we're in range. Maybe you can get more information on the situation to the north. You have a base station, right?"

"Sure," Jeff said. "I have a good antenna, so we should be able to keep in touch for quite a while. I'll find out whatever I can about the areas you're passing through and relay it to you."

The men shook hands.

Robbie and Katy both hugged Neil and said goodbye. They watched as he tightened his pack straps and started out again on foot.

Peter climbed behind the wheel and started the engine while Jeff got in the passenger side. Robbie and Katy squeezed into the extended cab back seat with Jackson. It was a tight fit, but nobody complained.

Robbie glanced back to see Rodney lying in the truck bed with layers of duct tape covering his zip-tied wrists, knees, ankles, with one more patch across his mouth. A tie-down ran through his belt and secured him to the bed of the truck. He wasn't going anywhere.

"KE7KFT," Jeff said into the truck's radio microphone, "this is NM8J. Everyone is safe and we're heading home now."

"Thank God!" Marie cried instantaneously. "Hurry up. Be careful. I'll monitor."

Jeff turned to Robbie and Katy.

"You were lucky. We all were. That guy had his act together. I'm glad you found him."

"He found us, thank God," Katy said.

"Neil, you still there?" Jeff transmitted. There was no reply. Robbie leaned forward in his seat.

"Did anyone get his call-sign?"

"Yes, I wrote it down," Jeff said. "We can try again from the house, where we have a better antenna. And we owe him a personal visit once this is over. He just made some life-long friends today."

"We all did," Katy added. She bumped her shoulder against Robbie and grinned at him. "You're my hero."

Robbie blushed.

Epilogue

"What frequency is Renee on?" Robbie asked. He sat perched in front of his father's radio. The signal was crystal clear, due to the tall antenna perched high on their chimney.

Neil gave him the frequency and they switched over.

"Neil, can you hear me?"

"Yes," Neil replied. "See if you can reach Renee."

"Renee, are you there?" Robbie called. "My name is Robbie, KE7CTA, and I'm calling for Neil. He's OK but not close enough to reach you yet. Can you hear me?" There was no reply.

Robbie repeated the message.

"Well?" Neil called. "Could you hear anything?"

A burst of static erupted from Robbie's radio. Robbie paused.

"Renee, are you there?" he called again.

"This is Renee!" an excited woman's voice called back. "Thank God! You talked with Neil? Are you sure he's OK?" The signal was weak, but still audible.

"Yeah, he's on his way home now. Hold on a sec, because he's on this frequency too. He can hear me but he can't hear you. Go ahead, Neil."

"Tell her I love her," Neil said. "Ask if she's OK. Does she need anything? Ask if she wants me to stop and get milk and eggs."

"He says he loves you, wants to know if you're OK, and if you need him to get milk and eggs on the way home," Robbie dutifully relayed.

Robbie heard Renee laughing, and then she sniffled. "Everything's OK here. I'm OK, the dog is OK, and the neighbors are OK. Tell him I love him too. How long before he gets here?" Robbie relayed again.

"Late tonight or tomorrow morning," was Neil's reply. "Can we talk a bit longer? Do you mind, Robbie? I just want to talk with her a little more. I wish I could hear her voice, but you'll have to do for now."

Robbie pictured the man who'd rushed in to help a couple of people he didn't even know.

"We can talk as long as you want."

END

Bonus Content

Welcome to the bonus content section. You may have questions about ham radio, emergency preparedness, wilderness survival, and more. Get some answers here!

Also, go to www.PreparedBlog.com and www.EmergencyCommunicationsBlog.com for additional free tips, updates to nonfiction content, and more!

All of the items in this section are listed in the order they appear in the story.

Enjoy!

[1] **What will work when the power goes out?** While visiting a friend, I commented on his new, low-flow, power-assist flush toilet. It used an electrically powered pump to flush more forcefully, conserving water. When I asked "How will you flush it if the power goes out?" he replied "I don't know."

Do you know what will work and what won't if your power goes out? If you're lucky enough to live in an area that hasn't experienced a power outage in a long time, you should consider shutting off your power for a couple of hours as a very simple disaster preparedness exercise.

[2] **What are butterfly strips?** Butterfly strips, butterfly bandages, and Steri-Strips (3M's brand name) are also known as butterfly stitches. They are thin, adhesive wound closure strips used to pull the skin together on each side of a cut. Sometimes they can be used instead of sutures. These very thin, narrow strips take up almost no space in a first aid kit, and are far more effective than adhesive bandages (or Band-Aids) in some cases. Adhesive bandages are usually designed to cover a wound, while butterfly strips are designed to pull a wound closed. Butterfly strips should be part of every comprehensive first aid kit.

[3] **What kind of flashlight should you get?** Nowadays, most flashlight packages show a lumen count as part of their marketing. How many are enough? Is it always better to have...more? Ask a flashlight geek. Yes, some people really enjoy building, modifying, playing with high-performance flashlights. See www.candlepowerforums.com for many examples. It's a great place to learn flashlight brands you've

probably never heard of before, uncommon battery types, terms such as spill and throw, and more. Back to the original question: how many lumens? It's a trick question. Many flashlights also have more than one option, and that's what I recommend. For general use, get a light that allows a low and high setting, with the high setting of 100 lumens or more, so you can use it at some distance, especially outdoors. The low setting is convenient if you need to look for something in the dark without ruining your night vision, or if you need less light for a much longer duration. I find that most of the time I only need five or ten lumens, but there are times (e.g. outside at night, versus inside at night) when I would rather have 300 or 500 lumens.

[4]**Will my cell phone work after a disaster?** Cellular phone companies *might* have portable, emergency equipment available in your neighborhood or region, which could be deployed after a disaster. And many cell phone towers have backup power sources, in case of a temporary loss of power. But even if your area might be covered, service would probably be limited at best. You should not assume that any emergency cellular service will be available in an emergency. Make sure you have a backup communication plan.

[5] **What kind of boots should you have?** Do you have hiking boots to use in an emergency, if you need to walk home (or anywhere else) when your vehicle is no longer available? If so, consider these factors:

1) Weight: heavy boots will kill your feet, joints, and back. Usually, the only reason to use heavy boots is if you're in unstable terrain (e.g. climbing in loose rock, up a mountain), or if you're also carrying a very heavy pack and need the additional

support. When you make your contingency plans, focus on a lightweight pack and lightweight boots.

2)   Practice: Use your boots, whether hiking, practicing your "get home" route, or just strolling around in the neighborhood, to make sure they're broken in. The last thing you need is a bunch of debilitating blisters when you're trying to manage an emergency situation.

[6] **Where can you find more information on fault lines?** If you live along or near one or multiple fault lines, as do many people in the Seattle area, you should determine what your exposure might be during an earthquake. Many research options exist online, and they make it easy to learn more. Start with a search at www.USGS.gov or your favorite search engine using terms such as "[your state] earthquake map".

[7] **Take care of your feet.** If you've ever been on a long hike, you understand the importance of healthy feet. Dry socks, the opportunity for your feet to rest and breathe, and paying immediate attention (e.g. moleskin or new socks) to any hot spots or blisters are essential to keeping your feet happy in a long-distance trek.

[8] **Can you use an amateur radio to transmit on FRS/GMRS frequencies?** Usually not. Katy's first radio is an AM/FM, NOAA, FRS/GMRS radio. Very few amateur radios allow for all of those bands to be combined with ham bands, which is why she has two. It would be handy if all amateur handheld radios combined all of those bands, but as it stands currently, the FCC generally makes that difficult.

⁹ **What are "simplex" and "duplex" communications?**
"Simplex" refers to communication from one radio directly to
another, without a repeater in between. The alternative is
"duplex," the mode used when speaking through a repeater.

¹⁰ **What's a "stubby" antenna?** In this case, it's a very short
and relatively inefficient antenna that can replace the stock
"rubber duck" (which is also inefficient and should be replaced
in most cases) or fancy, aftermarket antenna. Why would you
want a stubby antenna? At times, you may need to communicate
with someone nearby but not within earshot. A very short
antenna, especially when attached to a very compact radio, can
be much more convenient to carry and use. It's a convenient
option, but certainly not a higher priority than an efficient,
aftermarket antenna.

¹¹ **What is a Nifty Guide?** Nifty Guides are the aftermarket,
laminated manuals or quick-reference cards written by Bernie
Lafreniere, N6FN. He designs his guidebooks to be more
compact and easy to read and use than the often cryptic, long and
very dry manuals that accompany radios. I have one for almost
every radio I own and advise you do the same, unless you have
a far better memory than I do and can remember all of the ins
and outs of your radio's operation. In addition to improving
manuals, Bernie also makes small, laminated, folding quick-
reference cards that summarize the most important aspects of
operating a radio, e.g., how to enter a new frequency, set up a
radio for repeater operation, and enter a frequency into memory.
I like to keep one of these under the belt clip of my handheld
radio.

[12] **What is a calling clock?** A calling clock is a document specifying contact information and times or calling windows to be used in certain situations. If you have an emergency communications plan, you need a calling clock (and hopefully have one already). You can find more information on creating your own at www.EmergencyCommunicationsBlog.com.

[13] **What is one of the most important skills a new ham should master as a new ham?** Let's be honest. Many ham radios, whether handheld, mobile (designed to be installed in vehicles) or desktop-style, are not very user friendly in many ways, including a scenario as basic as programming new frequencies into memory. More experienced hams, especially those who participate frequently in public service events and emergency communications drills, are familiar with their radios and how to program them, but many will also admit that they have more than one radio, and since they're all different, it's a challenge to remember how each one works. So what do many of them do? They keep a cheat-sheet or guide handy! Note: some newer radios (finally!) have more intuitive user interfaces, and some even provide (gasp!) a USB connection to your computer. So they are getting better, albeit very slowly. In any case, *one of the critical skills a new ham should master is how to enter and store a frequency in his or her main handheld radio.*

[14] **Should you replace your stock antenna?** Absolutely. You have many options when it comes to replacing the inefficient antenna that comes with any handheld, ham radio. Some of those options are very flexible. Why risk damaging a long, rigid antenna when you can get a flexible one instead? In addition to being much harder to damage, you can place your radio in a smaller space if needed (though I don't recommend

171

this for long-term storage – you could put too much stress on the antenna connector), or detach the antenna and store it in a smaller space. Good antenna brands include Comet and Diamond.

[15] **What is a propagation test?** It sounds technical, doesn't it? It's nothing more than measuring to see whether a radio signal can reach another radio, and it's especially useful to do along your route home, if you plan to use radios for emergency communication. Here's a very simple approach you can take. Turn on a radio at home and a radio at work. The driver starts transmitting and driving, describing landmarks along the way, every few minutes (depending on the terrain and signal strength). The person on the other end transmits back and since he or she isn't driving, takes notes to identify which areas along the route have the best signal strength (where it sounds most clear). At the end of the exercise, you'll have a map that shows where you can expect to communicate effectively, and where "dead zones" (where the signal can't bridge the gap) exist.

[16] **What is a dipole antenna?** A dipole antenna is a long antenna, with two elements (like arms) that are usually positioned horizontally, like the top of the letter "T", with one element extending to either side of the vertical leg. The vertical leg of the "T" is usually a piece of coaxial cable (also known as feedline), which connects the top of the "T" to the radio. (A dipole can also run vertically, but in this case we'll use the common, horizontal example.) Dipoles are popular because they're easy to make, relatively easy to set up (there are entire books on this topic), and they work very well within a specific frequency range. They are usually very efficient. For example, if you want to listen and/or transmit on a specific band, like the 80-meter band, you can use a dipole antenna that is sized (or

"tuned") just for that band. If you'd like to learn more about antennas, you can find some great options at www.ARRL.org. One of my favorite books on antennas is "Low Profile Amateur Radio", but at the time of writing appears to be out of print. However, it is still available on Amazon.com.

[17] **Why do hams say "CQ"?** "CQ" is what hams say with voice, Morse code, or other digital transmission modes in some cases, as a way to ask "Who's out there on this frequency? Would you like to chat?", or "calling all stations."

[18] **What is NVIS, and why would you want to use it?** You can impress all of your friends with cool ham abbreviations like "NVIS." (It's often pronounced "en-viss," but you might also hear it pronounced "ne-viss" in the eastern US.) OK, you probably won't impress anyone. But you should know how it's used. Most often, it's used by people who want medium-range communications. If you don't have access to a repeater (or if you expect your local repeaters to be busy or off-line in a serious emergency), broadcasting HF signals vertically (versus more horizontally, as with most HF antennas) allows them to reflect straight back down in a circle with a diameter of around 400 miles. You can read more about NVIS at www.EmergencyCommunicationsBlog.com. Here is a very short description of some common ham radio communications methods:

- Local communications: UHF & VHF (simplex and repeaters);
- Medium-range, regional communications: UHF & VHF repeaters, HF NVIS;
- Long-range communications: Traditional HF.

¹⁹ **What are FRS/GMRS radios?** The initials stand for Family Radio Service / General Mobile Radio Service. The common "walkie-talkie"-type radios you can find at your local outdoors or sporting goods stores are usually this type. They operate in the UHF range, have limited range, are very common and can be relatively inexpensive. For much more information on the pros, cons, and other details, please read the chapter dedicated to this topic in my book "Personal Emergency Communications."

²⁰ **What is CERT?** CERT is an organization of volunteer emergency workers, and stands for "Community Emergency Response Team." It's also referenced in more detail in the novel "The Road Home."

²¹ **What is triage?** Triage is a fast, simple way to categorize patients, to ensure that people with life-threatening injuries that can be treated are treated first, and those who can survive on their own without treatment wait until the more important issues are addressed. The colors used in CERT usually fall into these groups:

- Green: able to walk and talk, any may have minor, non-life-threatening injuries;
- Yellow: needs urgent care, but it can be delayed up to an hour;
- Red: needs care immediately in order to prevent death;
- Black: dead or very near imminent death.

²² **Where can one learn more about "Map Your Neighborhood"?** See the article here, with additional links and

details: http://preparedblog.com/how-to-set-up-and-run-a-map-your-neighborhood-program.

[23] **Why should you consider an inverter generator?** Many (if not all) new inverter generators often have "economy" settings, which enable lower fuel usage when less power is needed. This is an obvious advantage in an emergency situation. Another benefit of the inverter generators is that they produce "clean power" (e.g. a pure sine wave, versus a square wave or modified square wave). This means you can power any devices (assuming your generator produces enough power) without worrying about ruining motors or sensitive electronics, which could be an issue with some non-inverter generators.

[24] **Where can one learn more about message handling?** If you think you'll need to understand, pass along, or receive formal emergency messages, then you should be familiar with this format. For a good write-up of how to use a radiogram, with additional resource links, try these two articles: http://www.amateurradio.com/the-arrl-radiogram-part-1, http://www.amateurradio.com/the-arrl-radiogram-part-2.

And the current, definitive guide to the format is here: http://www.arrl.org/files/file/Public%2520Service/MPG104A.pdf.

[25] **What's in a Get Home Plan?** A Get Home Plan will help you think methodically about how you'll travel home in an emergency, and describe the resources you will need, what you may need to store at work and/or in your vehicle, how you will plan to communicate and with whom, and more. You can find out more about putting together a Get Home Plan at www.PreparedBlog.com.

26 Can anyone have and use lock picks? Only locksmiths, burglars and the CIA use lock-picks, right? Wrong. Lots of people have fun picking, and they do it completely legally. Some do it for the puzzle-solving fun, as a hobby. And some do it just in case they might really need to unlock something and might not have the key. Of course, you will need to be certain about the laws in your area, but in many areas, having a lock pick kit is perfectly legal, and you can probably imagine the many, ethical uses for such a kit. For example, you could have lost your key to the lock on your backyard shed. In a disaster scenario, you can probably imagine many more examples.

27 Has anyone really done this? For a true story of a politician using this approach at a bus stop in Israel, especially if you like hard core self-defense books, you can read "Secrets Of Street Survival - Israeli Style: Staying Alive In A Civilian War Zone" by Eugene Sockut. Some of his ideas will probably get you in legal hot water in the U.S. and many other countries, but they will give you some good food for thought.

28 A worthwhile radio accessory: belt clip. Have you ever needed to walk around while holding your handheld radio or scanner? After a while, unless you're using it every several seconds, you'll probably want to free that hand to do something else, or you may just get tired of holding it. Many radios come with belt clips. Some are sturdy and some are pretty flimsy. In any case, test yours out. If yours isn't very sturdy, consider getting a separate radio holder that comes with a sturdy belt-clip. You'll really appreciate it when you need both of your hands free.

29 Think before you speak. Being clear and concise is a good idea any time you are using the radio; give a moment's thought to your message before you deliver it. Since radio communications are one way at a time, it's different than a phone conversation when you can both speak and hear each other at the same time. Especially in an emergency, you should try to say the most important things in the shortest amount of time, as clearly as possible, and then give the person listening a chance to reply and clarify if needed. This will take practice, so take advantage of an emergency communication group's weekly radio net in your area and check in as a guest, if you're not a member already. It's a great way to learn how to communicate in an organized, concise way. Remember, the best way to learn is to get on your radio and use it!

30 Can you use expired pepper spray? You can, but don't depend on it! Is your can of pepper spray ten years old? Replace it! That stuff doesn't last forever, no matter how high the quality. Take the old one and practice with it. Aim at something approximately face-high, like a paper plate tacked to a tree, and give a few, short bursts. Just as with your radio, use your tools. Get to know how far your spray/foam/fog travels, spreads out, how well it works in a breeze, etc. And follow the manufacturer's recommendation for freshness.

31 What is a Spyderco? Spyderco is a high-quality knife manufacturer, well-known for the innovative circle cut out of their folding knife blades. This ergonomic feature allows you to easily and safely open your knife with one hand, which is obviously handy when you're busy holding something with the other hand. The Spyderco Delica, one of my favorites, has been one of their most popular models for over twenty years, comes in a variety of styles, colors, and steel types, and easily clips to a pocket or waistband.

32 Why would you need a street map for an area you're already familiar with? If Jeff and his family live in Bellevue, do they really need a street map? Even if you have lived in an area for many years, you should still have an up-to-date street map. Unless you live in a small town or rural area, you will probably not know every single street (unless you work as a taxi-driver), and you may need to use unfamiliar, alternate routes in or out of an area if trees or bridges fall, or roadways become blocked for any other reason. High-quality, detailed local and regional maps are an important part of disaster preparation, so get one if you don't have them already.

33 Do you need a key ring flashlight? Is there any reason to *not* have a small, bright, long-life, reliable flashlight on your key-ring? That's easy: no. The Photon Micro-Light is a great one. I've had one on my key ring for many years. It's small, relatively flat, and it's always been reliable. You may prefer a different size or brand. Other high-quality examples include the Streamlight Nano and various small lights by Inova. Do your research, find one that works for you, and the extra light source will serve you well.

34 What is an azimuth? An azimuth is a line at a certain angle. The term is commonly used in orienteering and land navigation (especially when using a magnetic compass and a paper map, versus simply following a trail on a GPS), and it's a good one to understand. It's defined as the "horizontal angle of bearing: the angular distance along the horizon between a point of reference, usually the observer's bearing, and another object."

In this case, it's the line between Robbie's location on the tower and the horizon, along the 52 degree mark on the compass.

[35] **What is "dual receive"?** Some radios have dual receive functionality. This means they have two independent receivers, and can listen to two frequencies simultaneously. The ability to listen to two things at once may be useful, depending on your operating needs. For example, with some radios, you can scan one frequency band while continuously monitoring a specific frequency in another band. In other words, you could listen for a friend to call you on a specific frequency while trying to find traffic on multiple, other frequencies at the same time.

[36] **Why does pepper spray work?** Pepper spray's active ingredient, Oleoresin Capsicum (or capsaicin) is organic. This means your body will absorb it, versus immediately rejecting it (which is what happens with tear gas). Unfortunately, once your body senses that it has absorbed the substance (and that it feels like burning), it's too late, and your body had to metabolize it in order to make it go away, which typically takes anywhere from 20-45 minutes. That's why the effects of pepper spray last so long.

[37] **What good is povidone-iodine?** Povidone-iodine, also known by its brand name Betadine, is usually good to use as a wound disinfectant. I'm not a doctor, and I'm not giving you medical advice, but in interviewing a medical expert, I've learned that it is an excellent way to disinfect a wound shortly after the wound has occurred. You shouldn't use iodine in a wound after it starts to heal because it will slow the healing process, but shortly after a wound occurs, iodine is a great way

to disinfect. In addition, if you have a choice, povidone-iodine is a slightly better disinfectant than tincture of iodine.

[38] **What kind of trauma dressing should you have on hand?** The Israeli bandages are relatively popular, and they are effective, especially if you're putting a bandage on someone else, or using both hands to put a bandage on your leg, for example. However, if you want a bandage you can put on with more ease, i.e., you can apply it one-handed to your other arm, try the NAR (North American Rescue) Emergency Trauma Dressing. But don't take my word for it! Get one of each and test them, on your own arm, your own leg, someone else's arm or leg, and see which one you prefer. If you're not sure how to use them, do an Internet search for instructional videos on the brand you have. www.YouTube.com has dozens of examples. Personally, I prefer the NAR bandage. There are no clips to mess with and I found it very simple and intuitive to use. I can also use it by myself if I need to. Give it a try and see which one *you* prefer.

[39] **Do you have a good water filter?** The Sawyer brand squeeze filter is an incredibly simple, handy water filter, and the lightweight version only weighs three ounces. The latest version comes with three foil squeeze bags of different sizes, and believe it or not, they guarantee the filter for a million gallons. Sawyer uses the same hollow-fiber membrane filtering technology in other filters they market too, which are useful for larger groups of people, including gravity-fed drip-bags, as well as a kit that works with a five-gallon bucket. Aside from being handy while hiking or camping, these filters are a good disaster preparedness resource. Please note that if water is contaminated with pesticides, gasoline, or other chemicals, the filter will not remove them. That requires a different system (i.e., one that also uses

activated charcoal). This system is designed to remove biological contaminants.

⁴⁰ What else can you do with iodine? You can use many kinds of iodine, e.g. povidone-iodine, tincture of iodine, and iodine crystals to purify water. Iodine can serve as an effective, dual-use product, because it can be used for disinfecting wounds as well as disinfecting water. One recipe calls for 16 drops of 10% povidone-iodine per liter of water, which provides an iodine concentration of 8 ppm (parts per million), which will kill just about everything bad out there, including cysts, in 30 minutes (and will kill most viruses and bacteria in under two minutes). Note: Iodine will not remove chemical contaminants, but will kill biological contaminants. Do your research before choosing a solution that meets your needs.

⁴¹ Is a bag full of loot a good thing? Yes and no! If you're a pack-rat, then you'll need to use discipline when packing an "everyday carry" or "get home" or "three-day" bag. Why? Because if you don't control yourself, your back will have twice as much stuff as you need, adding extra weight and needlessly taking up space. For example, consider getting home in an urban or suburban environment. Do you really need two MREs in your get-home bag if you will only need to walk five miles to get home? Does your everyday carry bag really need three different methods of starting a fire if you live in the middle of the city? Do you really plan to have a campfire in the street? Does your urban survival kit include fishhooks, when the nearest lake is out of town? Do you need a backup shelter if you'll usually be surrounded by buildings? You should be ruthless when writing your equipment list, and to focus on dual-use items. Examples include duct tape (good for so many things, there are entire books

181

on just this topic!), a good multi-tool, a safety pin or two, and a length of cord. Remember, in addition to taking up space and decreasing comfort, more stuff means more weight, which means more calories needed to carry it around.

[42] **Why is a scanner useful?** While I've mentioned scanners in other books and blog articles, it's worth mentioning their value here. If radio is a form of communication being used in your area, whether by hams, law enforcement, bus drivers, taxi drivers, or anyone else, then being able to listen in gives you the ability to learn more about your environment. A scanner allows you to obtain critical information that could change the decisions you make, especially in an emergency. If you are serious about emergency communications, not only should you have a portable scanner available, you should be comfortable using it. No, you won't be able to intercept encrypted communications from your local SWAT team or the Feds. And you may have to decide whether to buy a more expensive model that enables you to intercept digital communications if your local government has updated (or will soon update – do your research) their systems to the latest standards. In any case, a simple analog scanner will still be useful for many more years. Any modern scanner should serve you well.

[43] **How can you get a custom call sign?** Neil's call sign K9NEL (not in use at time of publication) is a nice fit with his name. One fun thing you can do when you get your amateur radio license is to get a customized call sign, known as a vanity call sign. You can find more information here: http://www.arrl.org/vanity-call-signs.

[44] **Why should you pause?** A ham radio club in the Seattle area gives out an award at the monthly meeting, and it usually rotates between a few, long-winded hams. It's called the "Alligator Award," and represents the animal with a very big mouth and tiny ears. If you're talking on their repeater and "time it out," meaning you talk so long that you exceed the transmission limit, the repeater will automatically reset, cutting you off, and at that that point you would become eligible for the award. Fun aside, when transmitting on the radio, you should pause from time to time to let someone else break in. If they don't need to break in, then go on with what you were saying, but in addition to being courteous, it's common sense. It's easier to have a conversation, whether in an emergency or not, if you allow for pauses.

[45] **Why bother planning at all?** A common military adage reads "No plan survives contact with the enemy." This means the plan will need to change from the moment you start implementing it. So why plan at all? How does all this planning make sense, especially when discussing disaster planning or emergency communication planning, when you're practically guaranteed to have serious issues come up, issues you probably can't realistically plan for? There are many good reasons to plan. Here are two big ones:

1. If your plan involves other people in any way, it gives you all a common starting point. Even if things go haywire, you'll know that everyone using that plan will be starting with the first step, moving to step 2 or Plan B when needed, probably in the same way you are. It's not perfect, but it's better than having no reference point.

2. Creating a plan causes you, among many other things, to think about possibilities. It should at least reduce the number of complete surprises, and will probably also change the way you decide to prepare.

Don't fall into the trap of "Everything will be screwed up anyway, so I'm not going to bother with planning." Write up a basic plan for yourself and see what happens. Just writing the plan will give you new ideas and help you identify issues you hadn't thought of previously. You should see some value immediately.

46 Do you need to identify yourself with every transmission? Did you notice that a lot of radio conversations have taken place without each station identifying itself? Let's assume everyone has exceeded the 10-minute limit imposed by the FCC, and is in violation of the regulations. Are they really in violation? In most of the situations in this book, I don't think so. The FCC is clear about life and death situations. If someone is in danger and a radio needs to be used, use the radio and don't worry about the technicalities. Does that mean you can train without identifying yourself and without following other FCC rules? Absolutely not! If no real danger exists, then of course you should follow the guidelines. But in a real emergency, common sense should prevail and the focus should be on managing the emergency effectively, versus following every rule to the letter.

47 What's another reason to have FRS/GMRS radios? FRS/GMRS radios are quite common, as radios go, and useful across short distances. And they can be used by anyone, good or bad. That's another reason why it may be useful to have one (actually, you should have a pair) of your own. Aside from using it to talk to someone, it will allow you to listen to whatever is happening in your immediate area, regardless of whether you have an amateur radio license. Make sure you do a little research and get a model that will allow you to scan all FRS/GMRS frequencies. Many models have this functionality.

[48] **Would trap and skeet shooting useful in a self-defense situation?** You be the judge. Does it help you develop hand-eye coordination? Does it help you become more familiar with a firearm? Does it give you the opportunity to learn how to shoot accurately when under stress (even if the stress is "only" competition, a personal best, or a timer)? Of course, you won't see many people doing trap shooting with a home-defense shotgun, but I suspect you will see some very accurate shooting from avid trap and skeet shooters, whether it's from a fancy, sporting shotgun or a home defense shotgun. While trap and skeet is not the same as a taking a self-defense shooting course, some of the very same skills come into play, and if the mindset is right, it is a worthwhile way to train.

[49] **How should you handle a firearm safely?** Are Jeff's friends putting innocent people in danger, with multiple pellets from their shotguns missing the car and truck? Could innocent people be hurt? Maybe, but probably not. Since the road is clear, in this scenario it's very unlikely. They are experienced shooters, and are still making sure they don't hurt any innocents. While the story is fiction, they are following rule four of Jeff Cooper's non-fiction Four Firearms Safety Rules:

1. All guns are always loaded;
2. Never point your gun at anything you're not willing to destroy;

3. Keep your finger off the trigger until your sights are on the target;

4. Know you target and what's beyond it.

In this case, while they clearly intend to destroy both targets (which pose a clear, deadly threat to their friends), they also know the area behind the car and truck is clear; it's open road as far as they can see.

Note: There are multiple variations on these safety rules. If they're new to you, and you intend to ever handle a firearm, do a little research, familiarize yourself with all the variations, and take a firearms safety course from a professional trainer. Don't make excuses. Save up the money and make the time. If you're going to own and practice with a firearm (and if you own one, you should practice), be smart and make sure you know what you're doing.

[50] **What is a high quality red-dot scope option?** Aimpoint is a manufacturer of high-quality, long-lasting red-dot sights. By providing an illuminated dot to focus on, which indicates where a bullet will strike (at a certain range), these sights make it easier to acquire and hit a target while keeping both eyes open. The batteries can last up to several years, depending on the model, and they are usually incredibly rugged. They are expensive, some costing from $400 up to $1,000, or more. Other popular brands include Aimpoint, Eotech, Trijicon, and Leupold. Less expensive brands include Bushnell and Burris.

[51] **Why does some pepper spray have UV dye in it?** Many types of pepper spray sold for self-defense purposes contain a special dye that is only visible under ultraviolet light, used by

police to help identify suspects long after the effects of the pepper spray have worn off.

67809426R00108

Made in the USA
Charleston, SC
22 February 2017